Dionne nodded, but she didn't move.

Immanuel didn't either. Couldn't. Felt as if his feet were glued to the ground. Their eyes met, held for a beat. Lust exploded inside his body, threatened to consume him. Their connection was undeniable, but it was nothing he'd ever act upon. He'd been burned by love before, betrayed by a woman he'd thought was his soul mate, and he wasn't going down that road again. Not even for a dime piece like Dionne. He had to keep his head, had to remember that no good could ever come of them being lovers. *That's easier said than done*, he thought.

Dionne stared at him, her gaze strong and intense. His hands itched to touch her, to caress every slope and curve on her delicious body. His pulse quickened, and his thoughts ran wild. *What would she do if I kissed her? Would she push me away or kiss me back? Does she feel the chemistry between us, or is it a figment of my imagination?*

There's only one way to find out, whispered his inner voice.

Dear Reader,

Born into one of Italy's wealthiest, most prominent families, Immanuel Morretti has more money than he can ever spend. But that doesn't mean he's lived a charmed life. He is estranged from his father, has endured a bitter scandal that damaged his reputation and business, and he caught his fiancée in bed with another man—his younger brother. Love is the last thing on Immanuel's mind when he relocates from Venice to Atlanta, so imagine his surprise when he meets Dionne Fontaine and falls hard and fast for her.

Too bad she's off-limits.

On the outside looking in, Dionne seems to have it all, but she has fears and insecurities just like the rest of us. Unlucky in love, with two failed marriages, she's given up all hope of ever meeting her soul mate and living happily ever after.

Enter Immanuel Morretti.

The security specialist is more than just a handsome face and chiseled physique. He's the total package, a hero with a heart of gold, and everything about him excites her. Dionne and Immanuel are a match made in heaven. After a romantic weekend in The Emerald City filled with passionate kisses, shared confidences and delicious lovemaking, they decide to take a chance on love—and each other.

Hearing from readers is the highlight of my day, so keep the emails, reviews and messages coming! I appreciate each and every one of you, and I'm humbled by your support. Happy reading.

All the best in life and love,

Pamela Yaye

Seduced
BY THE HERO

Pamela Yaye

HARLEQUIN® KIMANI™ ROMANCE

Recycling programs
for this product may
not exist in your area.

ISBN-13: 978-0-373-86426-3

Seduced by the Hero

Printed in U.S.A.

Pamela Yaye has a bachelor's degree in Christian education. Her love for African-American fiction prompted her to pursue a career in writing romance. When she's not working on her latest novel, this busy wife, mother and teacher is watching basketball, cooking or planning her next vacation. Pamela lives in Alberta, Canada, with her gorgeous husband and adorable, but mischievous, son and daughter.

Books by Pamela Yaye

Harlequin Kimani Romance

Visit the Author Profile page at Harlequin.com for more titles.

Acknowledgments

This is my twentieth Harlequin novel. Yes, you read that correctly. TWENTIETH. It seems like just yesterday I got "the call," but it's been eight wonderful years.

They say it takes a village to raise a child, and the same can be said about publishing a romance novel!
I want to thank Harlequin, my amazing agent, Sha-Shana Crichton, for believing in my gift, past and present Kimani staff, and my friends and family for their unwavering support. I'm living my dream, and you're the reason why. Here's to twenty more!

Chapter 1

"Surely you can't be *that* dumb." Dionne Fontaine heard the scathing retort leave her mouth and wished she could cram the words back down her throat. Not because she felt guilty for losing her temper, but because the novice life coach with the Dolly Parton–like cleavage had burst into tears.

Her vice president and friend, Sharleen Nichols, glared at her as if *she* were the problem, and Dionne wondered if she'd been too harsh. Considering all of the facts, Dionne determined her next move. Sharleen and Annabelle Clark had arrived at her office ten minutes earlier, during her morning meditation time, and although she'd been annoyed by the interruption, Dionne had given them her undivided attention. She was the CEO of Pathways Center, the head woman in charge, and she prided herself on being accessible to her employees. Even starstruck life coaches who put themselves in compromising situations with male clients.

"Annabelle did nothing wrong," Sharleen insisted, her tone matter-of-fact. "It's not her fault Ryder Knoxx propositioned her during their free consultation yesterday. She shouldn't be blamed for *his* poor judgment."

Feeling contrite, Dionne spoke in a sympathetic tone. "Entertainers are notorious womanizers with no conscience. Since it's obvious Mr. Knoxx has a crush on you, I'll assign you to another client and pass the aging rock star on to a more seasoned life coach."

Panic flickered across her face. "No. Don't. I like him, and we have a lot in common."

"This isn't about you, Annabelle. This is about doing what's best for our clients."

Her shoulders drooped, and she slid down in her chair, as if she were trying to disappear into the plush, soft fabric. "But we clicked," she whined. "Ryder thinks we're kindred spirits."

Of course he does. He's trying to get into your pants, and you're too stupid to realize it.

Dionne struggled to control her temper. It was a challenge, especially in light of everything that had happened at the center in recent months, but she maintained her cool. "Your goal as a life coach is to encourage and support clients through their problems and issues, not become their BFFs."

Annabelle started to speak to argue her point, but Dionne silenced her with a look. Her Southern drawl was charming, but she was a pain in the ass and she wanted to get rid of her. "Life coaching is about helping people improve the quality of their lives without expecting anything in return," she continued. "It's imperative you act professional at all times, and don't, under any circumstances, accept money, gifts or favors from clients."

"Does that mean I can't attend the world music awards with Ryder next month?"

"That's *exactly* what it means."

"But—"

"But nothing," Dionne snapped, finally losing her patience. The more time she spent with Annabelle, the less she liked her, and she suspected the only reason the university graduate had applied to Pathways was to hook up with a celebrity. "You've only been working here for three months, and since you started it's been one problem after another…"

Sharleen tried to interrupt her, but Dionne was on a roll. She didn't believe in biting her tongue or sugarcoating the truth. She always spoke her mind. "I'm all for a woman using her physical assets to get ahead, but you need a make-*under*. Tone down the eyeliner, lay off the hair spray and, for goodness' sake, cover your tits. This is a place of business."

Sniffling, Annabelle cleaned her plump, tearstained cheeks with the back of her hands. "You're right, Mrs. Fontaine. I'm sorry. I'll do better, I promise."

"You better, or you're fired."

Sharleen winced as if she were in pain, but Dionne pretended not to notice.

"Pathways is my life, and I won't let you or anyone else destroy my agency."

Nodding, Annabelle rose to her feet and straightened her low-cut, belted dress. "I better head back to my office. My next session starts at ten, and I need time to prepare."

Annabelle hustled through the open door and closed it behind her.

Dionne was glad to see her leave. "You never should have hired her," she said, reaching for her oversize mug and raising it to her lips. "She's young and immature, and so damn gullible. It's hard to believe she's twenty-seven years old."

"Annabelle's a good life coach."

"That remains to be seen."

Sharleen released a deep breath. With her flawless complexion and delicate features, she'd always been a pretty girl, but since meeting race-car driver Emilio Morretti, she'd stepped up her fashion game. No longer self-conscious about the scars on her arms and legs she'd suffered in a tragic house fire, she'd traded in her dark suits for vibrant designer outfits. The oversize bow on the neckline of her red A-line dress was eye-catching, and her pearl accessories enhanced the femininity of her look.

"You're being too hard on her," Sharleen said.

"And you're being too nice."

"Leave everything to me. I'll mentor her and show her how to be a great life coach."

Dionne admired her optimism. Appointing Sharleen as her VP was the smartest thing she'd ever done. She hoped they'd be friends and partners for many years to come.

Not if Emilio Morretti has his way, whispered her inner voice.

The sports legend had proposed to Sharleen on her twenty-eighth birthday, and three weeks later she was *still* floating on air. Standing on the podium after winning the World Series All-Star Race, Emilio had stunned her friend—and the 1.5 million viewers watching worldwide—by popping the question on live TV. The happy couple were planning to exchange vows in Venice, Italy. Although Dionne had tried talking Sharleen out of getting married in December, her friend was determined to tie the knot in just three months' time. She was convinced Emilio was "the one," and she was so anxious to jump the broom, it was all she could talk about. Dionne only hoped Sharleen wouldn't one day regret her decision—

Like me, she thought sadly, swallowing hard. *If I had known then what I know now, I never would have married Jules after dating for only six months.*

"Annabelle has the requisite skills," Sharleen continued. "She just needs to put what she's learned in the classroom into practice, and I'm confident she can—"

"Well, I'm not. I think she's a liability, and I want her gone." Taking a sip of her green tea, she kicked off her Gucci pumps and reclined comfortably in her zebra-print chair. Dionne loved her office. It was bright, welcoming and feminine, just like her. She'd spent a fortune decorating it, and was thrilled her interior designer had brought her vision to life. Star-shaped chandeliers hung from the ceilings, teal walls evoked feelings of calm, her Versace furniture reeked of glamour, and the burgundy carpet was pillow-soft.

"Give Annabelle another chance. This is her first coaching job, and she's still finding her footing," Sharleen explained. "I believe in her, and you should, too."

Dionne drank her tea, gave some thought to what Sharleen said. "I liked you better when you were single," she teased, hoping to lighten the mood with a joke. "You used to be tough and tenacious, but now that you're in love you're a total softy."

A smile brightened Sharleen's face. It was obvious she was thinking about her fiancé. It took everything in Dionne not to roll her eyes to the ceiling when her friend sighed dreamily and gazed longingly at her engagement ring. It was the size of a golf ball, encrusted with diamonds, and it was the most beautiful piece of jewelry Dionne had ever seen.

"I can't help it," Sharleen said with a giggle. "I'm so freakin' happy, I feel like dancing in the streets. I want to share my happiness with everyone I know."

"I'm thrilled for you, but your romance is bad for business."

"Bad for business?" she repeated, arching an eyebrow. "In what way?"

"Because of you, our female life coaches are secretly hoping to make a love connection with every wealthy client, and as a result are breaking the employee conduct rules."

"My feelings for Emilio have nothing to do with him being famous, and everything to do with who he is as a person. He makes me feel special, as if I'm all that matters..."

They all do in the beginning, but it doesn't last. Trust me, I know what I'm talking about. I've been married twice.

"If Emilio lost everything tomorrow, it wouldn't change how I feel about him. I'd live with him in a cardboard box if I had to." Happiness warmed her face, and she laughed heartily. "But enough about me and my amazing fiancé. How are you doing?"

Dionne finished her tea and put down her mug. "Great, fantastic, couldn't be better."

"I know the last few weeks have been tough on you, what with your in-laws bad-mouthing you to the press and the construction delays at the Seattle and LA offices, but I'm here for you, Dionne. You don't have to deal with those issues alone."

"Thanks, Sharleen, but I'm fine, really."

"I don't believe you..."

What do you want me to say? "My whole world is falling apart, and if I didn't have Pathways to keep me going, I'd probably have a nervous breakdown"?

"It isn't healthy to keep things bottled up." Sharleen sounded wise, like a therapist counseling a distraught client. Her expression was filled with concern. "We're a team, and I have your back. No matter what. You can count on me."

Dionne shifted around on her chair and fiddled with the diamond tennis bracelet on her wrist. Every day, without fail, Sharleen asked how she was feeling, and every day, without fail, Dionne lied through her teeth. She didn't want to talk about Jules or their contentious divorce proceedings. Not with Sharleen. Not with anyone. Working helped Dionne forget her hurt, her failures, and she'd rather suffer in silence than pour out her heart. She admired Sharleen and thought she was an exceptional life coach, but a woman desperately and madly in love wasn't the right person to confide in. Neither were her two older sisters, Mel and Lorna, who both just didn't understand what she was going through.

No one does—that's why I keep my feelings to myself. Her gaze strayed to the window, and she peered outside. Pathways Center was in an attractive plaza filled with glitzy boutiques, cafés and beauty salons, but what Dionne loved most about the location was the hustle and bustle of Peachtree Street. Growing up in a large family, she'd always thrived in chaos, and having her business in a high-traffic area fueled her creative juices.

"We'll get through this together. You have my word." Sharleen reached across the desk and touched Dionne's hand, giving it a light squeeze. "If you need anything, just ask. I'm here for you, and so is the rest of the Pathways family. You've built a fantastic team, and any one of our colleagues would be glad to listen if you need to talk. We're a hundred percent behind you, Boss."

Dionne opened her mouth to thank Sharleen for her support, but she couldn't find her voice. She wasn't one to cry, but her friend's words made her eyes tear, and the room swam out of focus. *Good God, what's wrong with me? I'm an emotional wreck, and it's only ten o'clock.*

"How did your meeting go yesterday with Jules and his attorney?" Sharleen asked. "Are you any closer to finalizing the terms of your divorce? Have you finally reached an agreement you're both satisfied with?"

I wish, but he's determined to screw me over. Dionne's gaze fell across the picture frame on her desk. The photograph had been taken Labor Day weekend at her childhood home, and every time Dionne looked at the picture of her loved ones, her heart ached. In her culture divorce was frowned upon, something her deeply religious Somali father was vehemently against, and Dionne felt horrible about the pain she'd caused her family. Her parents adored Jules; so did her siblings, and every day her mother implored her to kiss and make up with her estranged husband.

No way, no how, she thought. Her Prince Charming had turned out to be a frog, and she was sick of playing the role of the dutiful wife. They were finished, over for good, and there was nothing Jules could say to convince her to reconcile. Their marriage had been stained with insults, name-calling and lies, and Dionne was ready for a clean break.

"Nothing's changed. Jules is still as stubborn as ever and…"

Dionne suddenly closed her mouth, stopping herself from saying any more. Even though she knew the divorce was for the best, discussing the demise of her marriage always made her emotional. Scared her emotions would get the best of her, and she'd end up bawling all over her Escada pantsuit, Dionne turned toward her computer monitor and typed in her password. "I have to finish my speech for the Seattle Leadership Conference, so let's touch base later."

"It's Thursday, remember? I'm off at noon."

"Hot date?" Dionne teased, playfully wiggling her eyebrows.

"You know it." Sharleen cheered and danced around in her chair. "Emilio's taking me to Fiji for the weekend."

"Again? But you guys were there Labor Day weekend."

"What can I say? My fiancé likes spoiling me, and I'd be a fool to stop him."

Enjoy it while it lasts, because things will change. They always do, and not for the better.

"I'll be back on Sunday, but call if you need me."

"Why bother? You never answer your phone after hours."

Her eyes twinkled, and a smirk curled the corners of her glossy lips. "You wouldn't either if you had a man to wine you and dine you."

"It's a shame Emilio doesn't have a twin," Dionne joked, laughing.

"He doesn't have a twin, but he does have five *very* single, *very* handsome brothers. Want me to hook you up?"

"Hell no!" she shrieked, fervently shaking her head. "The last thing I need is another lying, cheating man in my life. I'm better off alone."

"Not all men are dogs, you know."

You're right, they're not, but the good ones are rare and harder to find than the exit at a corn maze. Dionne hadn't dated anyone since leaving Jules and moving out of their marital home, and she had no intention of putting herself out there anytime soon. Her focus was on building her business and spending time with her family. They wouldn't hurt her, wouldn't betray her trust—

"You and Jules have been separated for almost a year," she pointed out. "Wouldn't you like to do something *besides* work? You're a great catch, Dionne, and there are plenty of eligible, successful men who'd love to date you."

"I'm not interested. I like my life just the way it is, thank you very much. I have my business, my family and my friends, and that's more than enough."

"Well, if you change your mind just let me know."

I won't, so don't hold your breath. Unconditional love

is a myth, and the notion of living happily ever after is a fairly tale.

The phone sounded, and Dionne sighed in relief. She was tired of talking about men, namely her good-for-nothing ex, and wanted to get back to doing what she did best: running her business. Dionne hoped it was her divorce attorney calling with good news, and placed her hand on the receiver to signal the end of their conversation.

Thankfully, Sharleen took the hint and rose from her chair. "Have a good weekend," she said, marching towards the door. "Don't work too hard."

Back in CEO mode, Dionne sat up tall and cleared her throat. Even though her marriage was in shambles, she looked forward to coming to work every day and enjoyed connecting with clients. "Dionne Fontaine speaking," she said brightly, turning away from her computer screen. "How can I help you?"

"You can start by returning the money you stole from me."

Her eyes narrowed, filled with hate. Damn. It was Jules. *Again.* How many times did she have to tell her assistant not to put his calls through? Her ex could be persuasive, charming even, but still Lily worked for *her*, not Jules, and now because her assistant was a softy, she was stuck talking to her estranged husband. The man who'd made her life a living hell for the past year. Her first impulse was to hang up the phone, which is what she usually did when he called, but this time she didn't. "I have nothing to say to you. Quit calling me at work. I'm busy."

"Return my money. You stole from me, and I want every cent back."

Dionne played dumb, pretending not to know what he was talking about. She was, of course, aware of what Jules was referring to, but she wasn't going to argue with him about the six-figure donation she'd made to the Atlanta

Children's Shelter just days before she filed for divorce. *If you can spend thousands of dollars at the strip club, then I can give thousands of dollars to a worthy cause.*

"This has gone on long enough," he snapped, his voice taut with anger. "You made your point. Now, move back home before I change my mind about giving you another chance."

"This isn't a game. We're through, and there's nothing you can say to change my mind."

"You don't mean that. Think of all the good times we've had."

What *good times? We argued constantly, and you betrayed me over and over again.* For five years, they'd lived in comfort and affluence, but it was time to end her marriage and move on with her life. Her parents couldn't talk her out of it; neither could her in-laws, and in the time they'd been separated, she'd never once regretted her decision.

"Every marriage goes through rough times," he said. "Don't let your insecurities ruin us."

"It was your lies that destroyed us, not me."

"We need to talk, *alone*, without our attorneys. What time will you be home?"

Her stomach twisted into knots. Was Jules in her house? Was he calling from her master bedroom? Snooping through her things again? Last Friday, she'd arrived home to find Jules in her living room, and if she hadn't pretended to call the police with her cell phone, he'd probably still be demanding she withdraw the divorce papers.

"If you keep harassing me I'll file a restraining order against you."

"But I love you."

Dionne burst out laughing. Surely he wasn't serious? Jules thought if he poured on the charm, she'd be putty in his hands, but his attempt to sweet talk her was so pathetic she rolled her eyes to the ceiling. His moods changed as often as the weather, and she'd always been on guard around him. She never knew what to expect, what would set him off, and hated how he used to take his frustrations out on her. "You don't love anyone but yourself. That's how it's always been, and you'll never change."

"If you come back home I'll buy you a Porsche, a new mansion, anything you want…"

Dionne tuned him out, losing interest in his smooth, slippery speech. Instead of trying to fix the problems in their marriage, Jules had put all his time and energy into running his family's construction business, Fontaine Enterprises. To this day Dionne felt as if she'd never truly known him. He had a temper, but it was his lies and infidelities that had destroyed their relationship. Despite his family pedigree and accomplishments, Jules was the most insecure man she'd ever met, and Dionne had no respect for him.

"Is this about money?" she asked.

Jules barked a laugh, and the sharp sound pierced Dionne's eardrum.

"Of course this is about money. With you it always is. Call off the divorce and I'll increase your weekly allowance by ten thousand dollars. Will that make you happy?"

Disgusted, Dionne stared down at the receiver with contempt. Jules was showing off, talking big, but she knew the real reason he was calling, why he was blowing up her phone day and night. Jules had political aspirations, dreams of being the next mayor of Atlanta, and feared a divorce would tarnish his perfect image. Dionne didn't give a rat's ass about his public persona. Reconciliation wasn't an option, never would be. It wasn't in his DNA to be faithful and honest, and she was tired of making excuses for his poor choices. Their marriage was broken, irrevocably damaged, and nothing could change that. "You know what would make me happy, Jules? A divorce. So revise your initial offer, or take your chances in court in November."

"I made you a generous offer, and I'm even willing to overlook the money you stole from me." His voice was terse, colder than ice. "If you embarrass me or my family in court I'll make your life a living hell, so I strongly suggest you think long and hard about your decision."

Dionne broke into a cold sweat and couldn't stop her hands and legs from shaking.

"Imagine what would happen to your business if the truth came to light."

Panic drenched her skin. Dionne had one regret in life, and it wasn't eloping at nineteen with her first husband; it was confiding in Jules about her past. He was threatening to tell the world the truth about her rags-to-riches success story, and his threats were weighing on her. On the surface, she appeared to be strong, but she was stressed out about the divorce and her future.

"You're not a self-made woman. You're a fraud, and if you don't do what I say, you'll suffer my wrath…"

Dionne was afraid of losing everything she'd worked hard for, but she refused to buckle under the weight of her fear. Jules didn't control her anymore, couldn't tell her what to do, and she was sick and tired of arguing with him. "This conversation is over."

"Like hell it is. It's not over until *I* say it's over. You hear me?"

"Goodbye, Jules. See you in court."

Without a second thought, Dionne dropped the receiver on the cradle, pushed all thoughts of her estranged husband out of her mind and got back to work.

Chapter 2

Two weeks. That's how long security specialist Immanuel Morretti had been trailing Dionne Fontaine. Always from a distance, he kept a low profile and blended into the background, wisely hiding himself in the crowd. He'd followed her husband's instructions to a tee, and was surprised to discover everything Mr. Fontaine had said about his estranged wife was true. She was curt, demanding and obsessed with her looks. Beauty treatments, shopping sprees and spa days were the norm. She loved dining at chic restaurants filled with socialites and celebrities.

Parked under a lamppost in a black Ford Expedition with tinted windows, Immanuel watched the front door of Pathways Center, keeping his eyes trained on the brick building in the middle of Peachtree Plaza. His company, Mastermind Operations, specialized in physical, personal and cybersecurity, and his surveillance division was in such high demand he'd had to hire additional staff last week. Since opening Mastermind Operations in Atlanta three months earlier, he'd been working nonstop—meeting prospective clients, training staff and creating innovative ad campaigns. But since Jules Fontaine had insisted Immanuel personally take on his case, he'd had no choice but to clear his schedule and leave his business partner, Malcolm Black, in charge. Jules Fontaine was not someone you refused, and Immanuel knew working for the esteemed CFO could open doors for him.

Immanuel had committed Dionne Fontaine's daily routine to memory. He'd collected a wealth of information since "meeting" her, but he hadn't uncovered anything incriminating yet. Her husband was convinced she was having an affair with a younger man, and he wanted physical evidence before their November court hearing. That gave Immanuel eight weeks to prove his worth to Mr. Fontaine, and he would.

Yawning, Immanuel leaned back in his seat and rubbed the sleep from his eyes. He'd been sitting in his truck for hours, but had used his time away from the office wisely. He'd read his emails on his BlackBerry, returned phone calls and spoke to his assistant at length.

His BlackBerry sounded, flooding his truck with light. Pressing Talk, he put his cell phone to his ear and greeted his cousin. "Hey, Nicco, what's up?" Immanuel lowered the volume on the radio. "How's married life treating you?"

"Great, coz, I couldn't be happier. You have no idea what you're missing."

"I think I do, and I'll pass. Marriage isn't for everybody, and it damn sure isn't for me."

"I felt the same way until I met my baby," Nicco said good-naturedly. "You'll change your mind once you meet Mrs. Right. You'll see."

Immanuel shook his head, snorted a bitter laugh. "Mrs. Right is a myth, so don't bet on it."

Nicco chuckled, and Immanuel did, too. He didn't talk

to his cousin often, only a couple times a month, but whenever they did, he had a good laugh. Now that he was living in the States, he planned to reconnect with his relatives, starting with Nicco and his brothers, Demetri and Rafael. He was looking forward to getting to know them better.

"How's Hotlanta treating you? Finally settled in, or still living out of boxes?"

Regret tormented his soul. After last year's scandal, he'd had no choice but to close down his offices in Venice. But not a day went by that he didn't think about his family, especially his grandmother, Gianna. They were close, and despite the mistakes he'd made in his past, she'd always been his most fervent supporter. "Dante found me a bachelor pad in Brookhaven, and as of last night I'm all moved in," he said. "I'm starting to like Atlanta—"

"Liar. You're homesick and anxious to return to Venice, aren't you?"

"Far from it. I have my hands full at the office and more work than employees." Immanuel had done his research, taken the time to explore the market, and realized the Peach State was an entrepreneur's dream. It had one of the strongest economies in the United States, and was home to prominent, influential businesspeople. Within months of opening Mastermind Operations, it was *the* agency to the stars. Thanks to his cousins' numerous connections, celebrities and entertainers were flocking to his agency for protection, and business couldn't be better. He had twenty-five employees on his payroll, and planned to double that number by the end of the year. He gave his staff the freedom to be themselves, encouraged them to think outside the box, and was reaping the dividends of trusting his team. Immanuel was contemplating opening a second location in Georgia, and had commissioned his younger brother, Dante Morretti, to find another property in Savannah.

"It sounds like business is booming. Tell me more."

Immanuel did. He told Nicco about his five-year plan, his latest ad campaign and the Fontaine case. It was the big break he'd been waiting for, and if everything went according to plan, he'd be doing business with Fontaine Enterprises for years to come. The Atlanta-based, family-operated company was one of the premier construction companies in the state. It owned dozens of local businesses and had plans to expand into other American markets.

"Jules Fontaine of Fontaine Entreprises? He's a big fish. How'd you meet him?"

"Through a mutual friend."

"I'm glad things are working out for you," Nicco said, his tone filled with warmth and sincerity. "And I'm looking forward to seeing you in December."

"You're coming to Atlanta for the holidays?"

"No, I'm going to Venice for Emilio's wedding. Aren't you going?"

Immanuel raked a hand through his dark brown hair, searching his brain for a suitable excuse. His sister, Francesca, had called him weeks earlier with the news, and as she chatted about Emilio and his fiancée, Immanuel got the sense that his brother had changed his life for the better. He was proud of him, but he didn't want to reunite with the superstar. "I can't go to the wedding. I have to work." He added, "You're an entrepreneur. You know how it is."

"Nothing's more important than family, Immanuel. Never forget that."

That's easy for you to say. Your kid brother didn't screw your fiancée.

"I called Emilio yesterday to congratulate him on his engagement, and he sounded great, all excited and amped up. His fiancée is obviously a miracle worker, because the last time I spoke to Emilio he was an emotional wreck."

And for good reason. Immanuel thought of Lucca, and

pain stabbed his chest. His nephew, an adorable five-year-old with curly hair and wide, expressive eyes, had died in a tragic pool accident at Emilio's Greensboro estate. The last time he'd seen his brother was at Lucca's funeral, and Immanuel cringed when he remembered the cruel things he'd said at his nephew's grave site. He'd let his anger and resentment get the best of him, and knew deep down he owed Emilio an apology. But he wouldn't attend his December wedding. Just couldn't do it.

"Coz, I have to go…" Nicco trailed off and didn't finish his thought.

Immanuel heard children's voices, laughter and a door slam.

"I told the kids I'd take them to Chuck E. Cheese's, and they're getting impatient."

"No worries, Nicco. Check you later."

"I'll call you next week. Love you, man."

Immanuel ended the call and plugged his cell phone into the charger. He picked up his energy drink and took a swig from the can. He glanced at his Rolex watch and frowned. Mrs. Fontaine usually worked until six o'clock, but it was seven forty-five, and he still hadn't seen any signs of her. Stretching, he leaned back in his seat and drummed his fingers absently on the steering wheel. Minutes later, the lights went out in Pathways Center, and the front door opened.

And there she was. The most beautiful woman he'd ever seen: Dionne Osman Fontaine. Immanuel bolted upright and peered through the windshield. The sidewalk was her stage, her own personal runway, and as she strode toward the parking lot with an air of confidence, desire shot through his veins.

His temperature soared to unimaginable heights. An erection grew inside his jeans. Immanuel was so aroused, so turned on by the sight of her, explicit thoughts crowded his mind. Thoughts of kissing her, caressing her and ripping the clothes off her sexy, curvy body. It happened every time he saw Mrs. Fontaine. His physical reaction to her embarrassed him, made him feel like a pubescent kid, rather than a thirty-nine-year-old man worth millions.

As he watched her, he took note of Dionne's graceful walk. She moved seamlessly, with a grace all her own. Every hair was in place, and her milk-white coat and black pantsuit made her look glamorous. He found it hard to believe she was thirty-five years old. She had the youth and vitality of a college-aged woman and the taut, toned shape to match.

Images of Dionne clad in a purple mesh top and spandex shorts were engraved in his mind. Four mornings a week, Dionne took a spin class, and watching her at the small downtown studio was the highlight of his day. The master life coach was exactly his type—strong, smart, independent, vivacious—but she was a diva. Someone who yearned for fame and fortune, and he was through hooking up with shallow, materialistic woman obsessed with the high life. *And besides, she belongs to another man. My client.*

His eyes trailed her every move. Petite, with creamy mocha skin, almond-shaped eyes and righteous curves, it was no surprise that everyone on the sidewalk stopped to stare. Her scarlet lips made her mouth look tempting, inviting, and thoughts of kissing her ruled his mind.

Knock it off, chastised his conscience. *Dionne's married to Jules Fontaine—a man who could ruin you in this town—and if you ever cross the line you'll regret it.*

Immanuel nodded to himself, knew it was true, but continued admiring the Somali-born beauty with the exotic look. Dionne had her briefcase in one hand, her purse in the other and her cell phone pressed to her ear. What else was new? She was addicted to her iPhone and couldn't go five seconds without checking it.

You're a fine one to talk, argued his inner voice.

Curious, he cocked an eyebrow. Immanuel wondered who Dionne was talking to. It was someone special. Had to be. Her eyes were bright, and her smile was radiant. Was her lover on the phone? The man her ex was convinced she was having an affair with? Immanuel hadn't found any evidence of her infidelity and suspected Mr. Fontaine was wrong about his estranged wife being promiscuous. She worked nonstop, even on weekends, and spent her free time at home—alone—not in bars and nightclubs.

Dionne stopped at the rear of her Lexus and popped open the trunk. Immanuel put on his seat belt and turned on the ignition. He didn't want to lose her in the parking lot, and reminded himself to follow from a distance as she exited the plaza. His cell rang, and he glanced down at the center console. His grandmother's phone number appeared on the screen. But he didn't have time to shoot the breeze, so he decided to let the call go to voice mail.

Immanuel looked up just in time to see a short figure clad in dark clothes approach Dionne. He scanned the man's face. The stranger had a desperate look in his eyes, a wild, crazed expression that was frightening, but Dionne was too busy talking on the phone to notice. He was pale and built like a defensive lineman. Immanuel read him like a book, sized him up in ten seconds flat. The guy was a thug, a no-good punk who'd rather rob than work, the most dangerous type of criminal. Immanuel had to act fast.

Sensing what was about to happen, he threw open his car door and took off running across the parking lot. The cold autumn wind sliced through his black button-down shirt, chilling his body to the bone, but he didn't stop. Couldn't. It was a matter of life and death, and he had to reach Dionne before the bastard attacked her, or worse, tried to kidnap her.

His breathing was heavy, ragged, and his heart was beating out of control. Feeling a surge of adrenaline, Immanuel ran faster, harder. Bent on reaching her, he dodged cars and wide-eyed strangers as he raced through the parking lot.

Immanuel heard Dionne scream, watched in horror as the man grabbed her and shook her violently. His stomach fell, plunged to his feet, and anger shot through his veins. What happened next stunned him. Dionne didn't comply with her assailant's demands, instead deciding to fight back. Kicked, punched, scratched at the stranger's eyes and face.

"Stop!" Immanuel shouted. "Get away from her. Let her go!"

The stranger knocked Dionne to the ground, grabbed her purse, and jumped into her car. Seconds later, he started the engine and sped out of the parking lot in her silver Lexus SUV.

Immanuel wanted to chase him down and kick his ass for assaulting a defenseless woman, but he couldn't leave Dionne alone. He didn't stop running until he reached her side. She was unconscious, lying motionless on the ground. Her face was swollen, her bottom lip was cut, and her designer clothes were stained with dirt.

Struggling to catch his breath, Immanuel dropped to his knees, gathered Dionne in his arms and searched the parking lot for help.

Chapter 3

Pain racked Dionne's body, stabbed every inch of her five-foot-two frame, making it impossible to move. She tried to open her eyes, but couldn't. Her limbs were cold, shivering uncontrollably, and her forearms ached. *Where am I?*

Sniffing the air, she detected the faint scent of flowers, and a delicious, masculine cologne that evoked thoughts of French kisses, red wine and dirty dancing. *Cologne?*

Panic soaked her skin. Her head felt groggy, as if she'd had one too many cocktails last night during happy hour. *Did I have a one-night stand? Did I follow some guy home from the bar? Am I lying in bed with him right now?* Dionne deleted the thought, refused to believe it, not even for a second. She'd never hook up with a random stranger, and besides, she'd worked at the office late last night, not gone for drinks at her favorite martini bar with her sisters.

Listening intently, Dionne soaked in the world around her. She heard the buzz and whirl of monitors and machines, a TV blaring, felt a coarse material rubbing against her skin. An intercom came on, and realization dawned. *I'm in the hospital. Why? What happened? Was I in a car accident? Did I crash my Lexus—* Before Dionne could finish the thought, memories flooded her mind. Leaving her office…someone sneaking up behind her…fighting him off…the crippling blow to the head.

Dionne struggled to get air into her lungs. It felt as though a bowling ball were sitting on her chest. Taking a deep breath, she broke free of the violent images holding her hostage. She wouldn't think about it. Wouldn't allow her attacker to victimize her in the privacy of her thoughts. Holding herself tight, she told herself she'd survived, that everything was okay. She was alive, safe, and he couldn't hurt her anymore.

With great difficulty, Dionne forced her eyes open. The room was bright, the air still and quiet. She lifted her blanket and gasped when she saw the cuts and bruises all over her body. The wristband on her left arm listed her name and health care number. More questions remained. Dionne continued to take in her surroundings. A wooden chair sat at the foot of the bed, a crystal vase overflowing with roses was displayed on the side table, and a tall, slim man in a black power suit stood in front of the window.

Dionne narrowed her gaze, sized him up. She needed to know who the stranger was and why he was in her hospital room. *Was he a cop?* Giving herself permission to stare, she admired his profile. The man was a force. A six-foot-six Adonis with olive skin, a full head of jet-black hair and a lean physique. He had specks of salt in his goatee and an imposing presence. He was a man of influence, someone who made things happen, who wasn't afraid of taking swift and decisive action. Dionne guessed he was in his thirties, but wouldn't be surprised to learn he was older. *Is he a doctor?* she wondered, noting his designer threads.

The stranger must have sensed her watching him, be-

cause he turned toward the bed and met her gaze. The faint
scar along his left cheek only enhanced his rugged, masculine look, and his piercing blue eyes were lethal weapons.

A slow, easy smile crept across his lips.

Dionne's heart skipped a beat, drummed in her ears. She
instantly recognized him, knew exactly who the drop-dead
sexy stranger was. He wasn't a doctor. He was a Morretti.
Had to be. No doubt about it. He had a straight nose and a
strong jawline, and looked like an older version of Emilio.

Months earlier, before things went south with her employee Brad McClendon, Dionne had researched Mastermind Operations online. She'd planned to hire Immanuel
Morretti's security company to help Brad find his estranged wife and sons. But since Brad had quit and taken
his celebrity clients with him, she'd changed her mind
about helping him reconnect with his family.

Dionne thought hard. She never forgot a name or a face
and recalled everything she'd read about the Italian businessman on his agency's website. He'd spent five years
in the Italian military in the special forces division, and
had worked for a decade as a personal bodyguard before
opening his security business in Venice. On the website,
she'd seen pictures of Immanuel with dignitaries, celebrities and high-ranking government officials, and according
to the Italian newspaper *La Repubblica*, his agency was
second to none.

"Good morning, Mrs. Fontaine."

He spoke with a thick Italian accent, one she was sure
drove women wild, but his expression was one of concern. Questions stirred her curiosity, made her wonder why
Emilio's brother was in her hospital room. Did Sharleen
send Immanuel over to check on her after hearing about
her attack? Is that why he was there?

"How are you feeling?"

Dionne cleared her throat and found her voice. "I'm

sore, and more than a little confused," she admitted sheepishly.

"My apologies. Let me introduce myself. I'm—"

"Immanuel Morretti," she provided, pulling herself up to a sitting position.

Surprise showed on his face, coloring his eyes. Immanuel looked rich, like the kind of man who dined nightly on wine and caviar. He carried himself in a dignified way. Thanks to her master's degree in psychology, Dionne was skilled at reading people, and instinctively felt the security specialist was someone she could trust. "You're Emilio's brother and the CEO of Mastermind Operations."

"You're a World Series racing fan?" he questioned, fine lines wrinkling his forehead. "I never would have guessed it."

"Emilio's engaged to Sharleen Nichols, the VP of my life coaching center. I've gotten to know him over the last few months. He's a great guy, and he treats Sharleen like gold."

Dionne watched his face darken, saw his jaw clench tight, and wondered what was wrong. *Are the brothers still estranged? Is that why Immanuel looks pissed? Because I complimented his brother?*

"Can I get you anything? Something to eat or drink, perhaps?"

"No thanks. I'm fine," she replied, shaking her head. "Where am I?"

"At the Atlanta Medical Center. You were robbed outside of your office last night."

Her eyes grew moist, and her lips trembled, but she willed herself to keep it together. "I remember," she said quietly. "But why am I here? I'm fine."

"You were unconscious when I arrived on scene."

"You were there? You saw what happened?"

"Yes, Mrs. Fontaine, I did." Immanuel glanced away

and slid his hands into the front pocket of his pants. "I was shopping at Peachtree Plaza when I heard a commotion and ran over."

"You scared off the assailant... You—you saved my life."

"No, I didn't. *You* did." His gaze was filled with awe, and it seeped into his tone. "To be honest, I came to rescue your attacker. You gave him one hell of a beating, and I was scared if I didn't intervene you'd kill him."

Dionne beamed, feeling a glimmer of pride at his words. "Serves him right for attacking me. He's lucky I forgot my pepper spray at home, or I would have emptied the entire bottle on him."

Like his voice, his laugh was pleasing to her ears and brought a smile to her lips.

"You're a brave woman, Mrs. Fontaine. A woman of incredible strength and heart, and you should be very proud of yourself. Few people would have been able to fight the way you did, and I'm blown away by your courage."

Moved by his words, she soaked up his praise. "Please, call me Dionne."

"Only if you call me Immanuel. All my friends do."

Her thoughts returned to last night, and dread flooded her body. Dionne was curious about what had transpired after Immanuel arrived on scene, and was hoping he could fill in the blanks for her. "What happened after I blacked out? Did the mugger steal my purse?"

"Yes, I'm afraid so, and your Lexus as well."

"Oh, no. My whole world was inside my purse. My wallet, my address book, my iPad." A chilling thought entered her mind. "The mugger knows where I live. What if he's at my house right now? Lying in wait?"

Immanuel strode over to the bed and took her hand in his. He was a calm and comforting presence. Having him nearby made Dionne feel supported and less afraid. She didn't know if it was because he looked like Emilio—a man she thought was considerate, compassionate and kind—or his warm disposition. But she liked his touch and drew strength from him. "I don't have a security system at my new place. I've been meaning to install one, but I've been so busy with work I haven't had the time."

"I know it's upsetting, but try not to worry. The police are investigating…"

What good will that do if the mugger attacks me in my sleep?

"I hope you don't mind, but I took the liberty of calling one of my technicians to change the locks at your house and office," he explained. "And if you'd like, he can also install voice-activated alarm systems at both locations."

"How do you know where I live?"

"I'm a security specialist. That's my job."

Dionne felt a wave of relief wash over her. "Thank you, Mr. Morretti. I appreciate it. At least I know the crook isn't in my house, robbing me blind." She was glad Immanuel was there. "Have the cops identified my attacker? Do they know who he is? Have they found my car?"

"No, not yet, but they assured me they're working hard on the case."

"Where's my cell phone? I need to call my family or they'll be worried sick."

Immanuel released her hand and stroked the length of his jaw. "I'm not sure if detectives recovered it at the scene, but you can ask them when they come to take your statement—"

The door swung open, and a slender fiftysomething nurse burst into the room. Her shoes squeaked as she approached the bed, and her frizzy white hair flapped around her face. "Good day, Mrs. Fontaine. How are you feeling this glorious afternoon?"

"Afternoon?" Dionne repeated, confused by her words. "What time is it?"

Immanuel checked his Rolex watch. "It's twelve fifteen."

"I've been sleeping for more than fourteen hours?" she asked, unable to believe it.

"You experienced a traumatic event last night and suffered a mild concussion," the nurse explained. "You need your rest, and for the next few days you'll have to take it easy."

Dionne didn't need rest; she needed a stiff drink, something with a shot of Patrón in it. But she knew her serious, no-nonsense nurse would never honor her request. "I'm thirsty," she said, touching her throat. "May I please get a cup of green tea?"

"Of course. Just let me check your vitals first. I wanted to do it earlier, at the start of my shift, but you were sleeping soundly and I didn't want to disturb you."

"You need your privacy," Immanuel said. "I'll wait outside."

No. Dionne opened her mouth to ask him to stay, but he was gone in the blink of an eye.

"Why did you fight back?" Detective Sluggs asked with a bewildered expression on his fat, fleshy face. "You could have been kidnapped, or worse, killed."

"No, *he* could have been killed, because I wasn't going down without a fight."

The emergency room doctor, a twentysomething brunette with Prada eyeglasses, scrunched up her nose. "I see cases like this every day, and it always amazes me that people are willing to risk their lives over something as trivial as a car."

"It's not about the car," Dionne shot back, annoyed that they were giving her a hard time about the choices she'd made last night. "I work hard for the things I have, and no one has the right to take them from me. *That's* why I fought back."

The doctor and the detective had entered her room ten minutes earlier, just as she was finishing lunch. But five minutes into the interview Dionne had already decided she didn't like either one of them, especially Detective Sluggs. He was curt and condescending, and his head was so shiny it looked as though it had been polished with Pledge. Dionne couldn't wait for him to leave. She'd had a busy morning and needed to rest. With the help of her nurse, she'd called the credit card companies, requested her accounts be canceled, then called her parents. She didn't tell them about the attack or that she was at the hospital, and had to cut the conversation short when her mom told her to make amends with Jules before their November court date.

"Fighting back only makes things worse," Detective Sluggs said. "You should have given the mugger your purse, handed over your car keys, and gotten the hell out of the way."

Dionne hit the veteran detective with a cold, dark stare. *Why does Detective Sluggs have to be such a jerk? Why can't he be sympathetic and understanding like Immanuel?* Taking a deep breath, she asked the question burning the tip of her tongue. "Is that the kind of advice you give your wife?"

"I'm not married."

Why am I not surprised? Of course you're single. You're a chauvinist pig, just like my ex.

"If you had cooperated with the perp, you wouldn't have been hurt," he continued, his tone thick with condemnation. "Next time you're tempted to do something heroic, don't, because it could cost you your life. A lot of these criminals are addicts, and the last thing you want to do is antagonize someone high on crack or crystal meth."

"Detective Sluggs is right," the doctor agreed, fervently nodding her head. "It's better to lose your car than to be beaten in the streets."

Dionne hung her head, stared down at her hands. Were they right? Had she acted reckless last night? Tears rolled down her cheeks, splashed onto her cheap blue hospital gown. But when Dionne heard Immanuel's voice in her head, she slapped them away.

You're a brave woman, Mrs. Fontaine. A woman of incredible strength and heart, and you should be very proud of yourself. Few people would have been able to fight the way you did, and I'm blown away by your courage.

"You shouldn't have been on your cell phone. That was your first mistake."

Her head whipped up, and her eyes narrowed. She felt her blood pressure rise, with the urge to smack Detective Sluggs upside his lumpy bald head. Orange *wasn't* the new black, and since Dionne didn't want to be arrested for assaulting a cop, she wisely kept her hands in her lap. "Are you saying the attack was *my* fault? That I'm to blame for what happened?"

Detective Sluggs made a sympathetic face, but his gaze was dark, and his voice was filled with accusation. "Perpetrators prowl the streets looking for people who are distracted, and you made yourself an easy target..."

Dionne pursed her lips so she wouldn't end up doing something stupid like cursing him out. Although she was annoyed, she gave the detective the floor to speak. And did he ever. He went on and on, spewing his opinions.

"I suspect this was a random, drug-fueled attack, but I want to cover all the bases." He flipped open his white spiral notebook and scanned the first page. "Mrs. Fontaine, do you have any enemies? Anyone who might want to hurt you or scare you?"

Do I have any enemies? Yeah, the entire Fontaine fam-

ily. Jules's older sister, Adeline, had never liked her, and the feeling was definitely mutual. The executive accountant was a control freak who wasn't happy unless she was calling the shots, and Dionne couldn't stand her. There was no love lost between Dionne and her in-laws, but they had nothing to do with the attack. "No, no one I can think of," she answered truthfully. "My husband and I are legally separated and in the process of getting a divorce, but Jules would never do anything to hurt me."

"Don't be so sure. Divorce brings out the worst in people."

Desperate to change the subject, she asked, "Where's my cell phone?"

"We found it smashed to smithereens in the parking lot last night."

Disappointment flooded her body, but the loss of her iPhone was the least of her problems. Anxious to end the interview and leave the hospital, Dionne addressed her doctor. "Have my test results come back?"

"Yes," she said, glancing at the sheets of paper attached to a metal clipboard. "Your CT scan was normal, and you don't seem to have any lingering effects from the concussion. But I'd like you to see the hospital psychologist before I discharge you."

"No, thank you. I'm fine."

"I strongly advise you not to leave. You suffered a traumatic event less than twenty-four hours ago, and it's imperative you speak to a professional to discuss the attack."

"I concur," Detective Sluggs said, stroking his bushy mustache with tender loving care.

Dionne glanced from the detective to the doctor and rolled her eyes to show her frustration. They were giving her a headache, and she was anxious to get away from them. Determined to leave the hospital, whether or not the doctor signed the discharge papers, Dionne searched the room for her clothes. Her Escada pantsuit was probably ripped and dirty, but it was all she had. Besides, she wasn't going to a black-tie event at the W hotel; she would be headed to her office. By the time she arrived at Pathways Center, her staff would be gone for the day, so she wouldn't have to worry about anyone seeing her bruised face.

"I have to return to the precinct, but if you remember anything else about the attack, don't hesitate to contact me." Detective Sluggs promised to be in touch and left the room.

Finally. I thought he'd never leave. Dionne checked the time on the clock. Immanuel should be back any minute now. For some reason, the thought of seeing him again excited her and made a smile balloon inside her heart. He'd spent the entire afternoon with her, and talking to him about her career had momentarily taken her mind off the assault. Though he was serious and soft-spoken, he made her laugh and told amusing stories about his life in Venice. He'd offered to go to the store for her, and Dionne eagerly awaited his return, because once he arrived with the items she'd requested, she was leaving. She was tired of being in the hospital and was anxious to leave, but first she had to get Dr. Pelayo off her back. "I don't need to talk to anyone," she said, speaking calmly, in her most serious voice. "I have a master's degree in psychology, and I know what to do to preserve my mental health. Now, kindly bring the discharge papers so I can sign them and leave."

The silence was so loud it drowned out every other noise in the room. Sunshine seeped through the window blinds, filling the drab, boring space with light, but it did nothing to brighten Dionne's mood. She was frustrated that Dr. Pelayo wasn't listening to her and was losing patience.

"Very well," the doctor said after a long moment. "If you insist."

"Thank you, Dr. Pelayo. I appreciate everything you and your staff have done for me."

"I'll have the discharge papers waiting at the front desk within the hour. Who will be picking you up and driving you home?"

Confusion must have shown on Dionne's face, because Dr. Pelayo continued.

"Someone has to pick you up upon discharge and escort you out of the building," she explained, tucking her clipboard under her arm. "The policy was put in place decades ago to ensure that all patients at Atlanta Medical Center remain safe after their stay—"

"I'm not a child," Dionne argued. "And I won't be treated like one."

The intercom came on, and the women fell silent.

Sitting in bed, doing a slow burn, Dionne pictured herself jumping out her fifth-floor window and running away from the hospital. *Who do I have to bribe to get the hell out of here?* she wondered, trying to keep her temper at bay. *And who came up with this stupid discharge policy? It's the dumbest thing I've ever heard, and I won't adhere to it.*

"I have to release you into the care of a loved one, preferably someone who can stay with you for the rest of the day." Dr. Pelayo's face softened with concern. "Victims often feel fearful after an attack, so it's important you're not alone over the next twenty-four hours. Isn't there a friend or family member I can call to pick you up?"

"I don't want anyone hovering over me. I'd rather be alone."

"I understand, Mrs. Fontaine, and I'm not trying to be difficult, but it's hospital policy, and if I break the rules I could lose my job."

Disappointed, Dionne collapsed against the pillows. *Will this nightmare ever end?*

Chapter 4

Dionne had no argument left in her and reluctantly gave up the fight. Arguing with Dr. Pelayo wasn't helping her cause, so she considered her options. She thought of calling a taxi to pick her up, but remembered she had no purse, no wallet, no money. Phoning her assistant or one of her senior life coaches was out of the question. She didn't want anyone to know about the attack and hoped to keep it a secret. Sharleen was in Fiji with Emilio, her sisters were home with their kids and her parents were at work. Though retired, they both worked part-time to stave off boredom, but Dionne knew if she called them they'd drop everything and rush to the hospital. The problem was, she didn't want them there. She felt ashamed, embarrassed that the mugger had attacked her, and wanted to put the whole ugly incident behind her as quickly as possible.

"Please reconsider calling your husband," Dr. Pelayo urged. "I understand that you're separated, but you need his love and support now more than ever."

No, I don't. I need a glass of Muscat and a hot bubble bath.

"Tragedies have a way of reminding us what's important in life and bring us even closer to the people we love. I think your husband would want to be here with you."

A sharp knock on the door drew Dionne's gaze across the room. Immanuel entered in all of his masculine glory and nodded politely in greeting. Dionne stared at him. So did Dr. Pelayo. The physician was wearing a dreamy expression on her face, one that indicated she was head over heels in lust. Immanuel had that effect on everyone—nurses, housekeeping, doctors—and seemed oblivious to the commotion he caused whenever he entered a room. That made him all the more appealing in her eyes.

"Sorry I took so long to return. Traffic was crazy on the freeway…"

He spoke quietly in a smooth, sexy tone. His voice was seductive, his cologne, too, and when their eyes met Dionne had to remind herself to breathe. He moved with confidence, like a man who had the world at his feet—and he probably did.

"How are you feeling?"

Better now that you're here, she thought, but didn't say. Immanuel was the calm in the midst of the storm, and Dionne was glad he was back. "Almost as good as new."

Immanuel was holding a shopping bag in one hand and a garment bag with the Gucci logo in the other. He placed both items on the bed. "These are for you. I hope you like them."

"What's all this? All I asked for was shampoo and body wash."

"You're going home today, and I figured you'd need something nice to wear."

The shopping bag was filled with sweet-smelling toiletries, everything from deodorant to scented oils and perfume. Dionne unzipped the garment bag, and a gasp fell from her mouth. A navy pantsuit, and a silk scarf were inside. Inside the shopping bag was a shoe box with black red-heeled pumps.

Dionne couldn't believe it, thought she was dreaming with her eyes open. How did Immanuel know her size? Who'd told him that Gucci was her favorite designer? She'd tried on the same outfit last week at Saks Fifth Avenue, but couldn't justify spending thousands of dollars on clothes when Jules was fighting her about money. Touching the lapel of the jacket, she admired the intricate design along the collar of the white ruffled blouse, then quickly re-zipped the bag. "Immanuel, I can't keep this. It's too expensive."

"It's a gift."

"But it cost forty-five hundred dollars."

"It doesn't matter," he said, his tone firm. "You had a rough night, and I think you deserve to leave the hospital in style. Don't fight me on this."

Dr. Pelayo's eyes lit up, and Dionne knew the physician was impressed. So was she. Not because of the staggering cost of the outfit, but because Immanuel—someone she'd just met—had done something kind for her, something her ex never did. Jules had relied on his secretary to buy her gifts, even had her sign the cards on his behalf, regardless of the occasion. *If Jules had been more thoughtful and attentive, our marriage wouldn't have fallen apart—*

"Have you been discharged?" Immanuel asked.

Dionne blinked and broke free of her thoughts. "No, not yet, but I'm working on it."

"Is there anything I can do to help?"

Before Dionne could answer, Dr. Pelayo told Immanuel about the hospital discharge policy and expressed her opinion on the matter. "Mrs. Fontaine is going to need a lot of emotional support in the coming weeks, so it's imperative she reach out to her friends and family for help," the doctor explained. "I'm trying to convince her to call her husband."

Immanuel turned to Dionne.

The heat of his gaze left her breathless and tingling all over. Dionne smoothed a hand over her hair, and winced when she felt tangles in her wavy dark locks. *Is that why Immanuel's staring at me? Because I look a hot mess?*

"Is that what you want? For Dr. Pelayo to call your husband?"

Hell no. Knowing her response would raise eyebrows, she swallowed her retort and shook her head. Dionne wasn't calling Jules, and she wished Dr. Pelayo would stop pressuring her to do so. Besides, Jules would never come pick her up. Work was all that mattered, all he cared about, and that would never change.

"I can drive you home."

Dionne met his gaze. "You can?"

"It would be my pleasure."

"Are you sure?" she asked, moved by his words. "You've already done so much for me, and I'd hate to inconvenience you."

"It's no inconvenience at all. I live in Brookhaven too, remember?"

"That's right, we're neighbors, I forgot." Dionne wanted to break out in song. Now she wouldn't have to bother her family to pick her up, and no one would ever know about the attack. Immanuel Morretti was a hero, a stand-up guy with a heart of gold, and Dionne was grateful for everything he'd done for her in just a short period of time.

A shiver whipped through her body. It frightened her to think what would have happened if Immanuel hadn't come to her rescue last night.

"I'll be back in an hour," Immanuel said, glancing at his gold wristwatch. "I'll go home, swap my McLaren for my SUV and meet you at the front desk at four."

"You don't have to go to all that trouble. I'm just grateful for the ride."

"Are you sure? It's a small sports car, and I don't want you to be uncomfortable."

"I'm positive," she said, blown away by his thoughtfulness. Dionne returned his smile, deciding right then and there that Immanuel Morretti was the most considerate, compassionate man she'd ever met, and she liked him immensely. "I don't know how I'll ever repay your kindness."

"You don't have to. I'm a Morretti, and we're not happy unless we're rescuing someone," he said with a hearty chuckle. Immanuel touched her hand and gestured to the door with his head. "I'll be in the waiting room. Take as long as you need."

As Immanuel and Dr. Pelayo exited the room, Dionne saw the doctor make her move. Resting her hand on his forearm, she leaned into him and spoke in a sultry whisper. *Is she giving him her number? Asking him out? Inviting him over for drinks?*

Dionne sat up and tossed aside the blanket. She told herself she didn't care, and that it was none of her business what they were talking about. But if that were true, then why did she want to jump out of bed and wrestle the pretty doctor to the ground?

"Sorry for making you wait, but I'm ready now."

Immanuel glanced up from the September issue of *Entrepreneur* magazine, saw Dionne standing beside the water dispenser in the hospital waiting room and felt the magazine fall from his hands. Desire careered down his spine and shot to his groin. Immanuel heard his pulse in his ears, pounding, thumping, and he swallowed hard.

Immanuel recognized he looked foolish, sitting there with his eyes wide, staring at her, but he didn't have the strength to turn away. Women who carried themselves with poise and grace had always been his weakness, and Dionne was the epitome of class. The Gucci pantsuit was made for her, created for a woman with her delicious shape. Her fresh face only enhanced her natural beauty.

"Immanuel?"

At the sound of his name, Immanuel snapped to attention. He picked up the discarded magazine, chucked it on the side table and rose to his feet. Smoothing a hand over his suit jacket, he crossed the room toward her. He started to speak, but her floral fragrance tickled his nostrils and his thoughts went off track. The hairs on the back of his neck shot up, and sweat immediately soaked his pale blue shirt. Her beauty was striking, and everything about her appealed to him—her confidence, her resilience, the way she carried herself. Over the years he'd provided security for pop stars, actresses and supermodels, but none of them could compete with the master life coach. But it was more than just her looks. She was a woman of strength and tenacity, and he greatly admired her. She'd fought for her life last night, gone toe-to-toe with a man twice her size, and survived the harrowing ordeal. "Dionne, you're gorgeous."

"It's Gucci," she said with a dismissive shrug. "*Everyone* looks great in Gucci."

"Your beauty has nothing to do with your outfit and everything to do with your smile."

A flush crept over her cheeks. "Thank you, Immanuel. You're very sweet."

And you're stunning. He remained quiet, cautioned himself not to speak his mind. Immanuel was glad he could help Dionne, but he didn't want to freak her out by coming on too strong. She had a presence about her, an intangible quality that intrigued him, and he was looking forward to spending the rest of the afternoon with her. Isn't that what Dr. Pelayo had suggested? That he keep an eye on her? Immanuel planned to follow the doctor's orders, though he wondered how Dionne would feel about him being at her house. "Shall we go?"

"Absolutely. I've been ready to leave for hours."

Walking down the hallway, Dionne moved at a slow, easy pace. She seemed to be favoring her right side, so Immanuel rested a hand on her back and led her into the waiting elevator. She smelled of lavender—his favorite female scent. They were standing so close, he wanted to take her in his arms and crush his lips to her mouth.

Guilt consumed him. Dionne was still legally married, which meant she was off-limits. Putting the moves on a vulnerable woman would be a boneheaded thing to do, so he dropped his hands to his sides. His infatuation with her was spiraling out of control, but Immanuel was determined to control his libido. *I'm horny as hell, but that's no excuse to put the moves on another man's wife,* he told himself, tearing his gaze away from her bottom. *I won't cross the line.*

On the main floor, Immanuel led Dionne past the hospital gift shop, through the lobby and out the sliding glass doors. His car was parked at the curb, and when he opened the passenger door for Dionne she smiled her thanks and slid inside.

Minutes later they were off. Having followed Dionne home from work countless times before, Immanuel knew where she lived, but since driving straight to her house would raise suspicions, he asked for directions. Dionne gave him her address, then turned her face to the window. She obviously didn't want to talk, so Immanuel didn't pester her with conversation. She'd suffered a traumatic ordeal, and despite her outward display of calm, he sensed that she was scared to go home. Immanuel didn't blame her. Her attacker was still on the loose, and the police had no leads.

"It's weird not having my cell phone," she said quietly, glancing in his direction. "I keep putting my hands in my pocket, expecting it to be there, but it's not."

"That's normal, especially for someone who uses their phone as much as you do."

"How do you know I use my phone a lot?"

Immanuel searched his brain for a suitable response, came up empty, and said the first thing that came to mind. "Most people do," he said with a shrug. "Myself included."

"My family thinks I'm addicted to my cell, especially my mom, but she's old-school and doesn't understand the nature of my job. I run my own company, so it's important to be available for my staff and clients..."

Immanuel didn't want to miss anything she had to say, so he turned off the radio and gave her his full attention. It was a challenge, with their arms touching and her heady perfume sweetening the air. But he listened closely and filed information away in his mental Rolodex for a later date.

"How long have you had your business?"

Pride filled her eyes and seeped into her tone. "It will be ten years in January."

"That's a remarkable feat. Most small businesses don't survive the first two years, so you're obviously doing something right."

"Damn right I am," she said. "I'm working my ass off!"

And what a nice ass it is.

"Well, if the life coaching business doesn't work out you can always become a boxer. You have one hell of a right hook."

Dionne cracked up. It did his heart good to hear her laugh. Talking to her about Pathways Center was obviously the way to go, so he asked questions about her business.

"What's your secret?" he asked, wanting to hear more

about her journey to success. The research he'd done on Dionne revealed that she was also a best-selling author and motivational speaker. She charged five figures for every speaking engagement, and was one of the most sought-after life coaches in the nation. "How have you managed to create a successful life coaching business when so many others have failed?"

"Hard work and perseverance are the keys to my success. I wouldn't be here today if I'd wavered, even for a second, about my life's purpose."

"Do you have plans to expand your business in other markets?"

The smile vanished from her lips. "My clinics in LA and Seattle were supposed to open this past summer, but construction has been delayed indefinitely."

"That's ridiculous," Immanuel said, shifting gears as he switched lanes. "Who's the builder, and why haven't you sued them for breach of contract?"

"Because my hands are tied." Her voice broke, cracked with emotion, but she quickly regained her composure. "This project was in the works long before I filed for divorce, but if I'd known my ex would deliberately sabotage the project, I never would have used his family's construction company. The project has been on hold for months, and work probably won't resume until the divorce is finalized."

"How long have you been separated from your husband?"

"Almost a year. Out of respect for his family, I agreed to keep quiet about the separation, but once I filed for divorce the story hit the newspapers and things turned ugly…"

Immanuel frowned. His thoughts returned to weeks earlier. During an hour-long meeting with Jules Fontaine, the businessman had called his estranged wife a conniving manipulator who used her looks to advance her career.

He claimed he'd kicked her out of their Buckhead estate once he'd learned of her infidelity. Immanuel liked having all of the facts and sensed that Dionne was telling the truth. She didn't bad-mouth her ex or blame him for their failed marriage. He respected her for taking the high road.

"Do you mind stopping at the AT&T store on Town Road?" she asked. "I'm expecting several important calls this afternoon, and I'll go crazy if I don't get a new iPhone."

"I don't know," he teased, faking a frown. "Dr. Pelayo ordered me to take you straight home, and I'd hate to get on her bad side."

"Don't worry. What she doesn't know won't hurt her."

Immanuel chuckled. "No problem. We can go anywhere you want."

At the intersection, he turned left and found a parking space in the plaza. They entered the store, and Dionne immediately selected the latest iPhone model, and then approached the cash register.

"With the extended warranty, that comes to $649," the clerk said.

Dionne nodded. "Charge everything to the account on file. I'll be keeping the same plan."

"In order to do that I'll need to see two pieces of ID."

"I don't have any ID. My purse was stolen last night." Dionne peered over the clerk's shoulder and motioned to the door behind him. "Is your manager around? I spoke to her earlier, and she assured me getting a new cell phone would not be a problem."

"I'm sorry, but she's gone for the day."

"Call her. I explained my situation to her, and she was—"

"I can't." He shrugged his bony shoulders. "Come back tomorrow with the proper ID."

Dionne spoke through pursed lips. "Go. Call. Your. Store. Manager. *Now.*"

"Ma'am, you're being rude. I'm going to have to ask you to leave."

Hoping to defuse the situation, Immanuel opened his leather wallet, took out his Visa Black Card and handed it to the clerk. "That won't be necessary." He was ticked off that the guy was giving Dionne a hard time, but he didn't let his frustration show. "Charge everything to my account."

"No," Dionne argued, adamantly shaking her head. "I don't want you to pay. All he has to do is call his manager. She'll straighten everything out."

"Don't worry, Dionne. I got this." Winking, he patted her good-naturedly on the hips. That earned him a smile. His chest inflated with pride, filled to the brim. "Hang tight. We'll be out of here before you know it, and you can go home and get some rest. I promise."

To reduce the tension, Immanuel chatted with the clerk about the weather and sports. The man was a huge baseball fan and screeched like a parrot when Immanuel told him Demetri Morretti, the star slugger of the Chicago Royals, was his cousin.

"The Royals will be in town at the end of the month," the clerk said excitedly, rubbing his hands together. "I can't wait to see Demetri play. I hope the game goes extra innings."

Immanuel chuckled. "Thanks for everything, man. You've been really helpful."

"Helpful my ass," Dionne grumbled, snatching the plastic bag off the counter.

"Thanks for choosing AT&T," the clerk said. "Have a nice day."

Outside, Immanuel opened the passenger door and stepped aside. But Dionne didn't get in. "You're too nice," she said, shielding her eyes from the sun. "This isn't Venice, Immanuel. This is Georgia. You better toughen up, or people will walk all over you."

"My grandmother, Gianna, says you can catch more flies with honey than vinegar, and I think she's right. So the next time someone's being a jerk, kill them with kindness. Trust me, it works every time."

"Maybe you're right."

To make her laugh, he joked, "I'm a Morretti. I'm *always* right."

Her smile was fake, forced, and seeing the wounded expression on her face saddened him. He'd said too much. She'd been through a lot in the past twenty-four hours, and the last thing Dionne needed was someone coming down on her. But before he could apologize, she spoke.

"I'm sorry if I embarrassed you inside the store. I didn't mean to. Because I'm petite, people usually don't take me seriously, so I have to raise my voice to get their attention."

"I understand, but don't stoop to *their* level. Let them rise to yours."

"Great advice. I'm going to remember that."

"Are you ready?"

Dionne nodded, but she didn't move. Immanuel didn't either. Couldn't. Felt as if his feet were glued to the ground. Their eyes met, held for a beat. Lust exploded inside his body, threatening to consume him. Their connection was undeniable, but it was nothing he'd ever act upon. He'd been burned by love before, betrayed by a woman he'd thought was his soul mate, and he wasn't going down that road again. Not even for a dime like Dionne. He had to remember that no good could ever come of their being lovers. *That's easier said than done,* he thought.

Dionne stared at him, her gaze strong and intense. His hands itched to touch her, to caress every slope and curve on her delicious body. His pulse quickened, and his thoughts ran wild. *What would she do if I kissed her?*

Would she push me away or kiss me back? Does she feel the chemistry between us, or is it a figment of my imagination?

There's only one way to find out, whispered his inner voice.

Chapter 5

"Immanuel, are you coming?"

Immanuel blinked, just then noticing Dionne sitting in the passenger seat of his car wearing a bemused expression on her face. He inwardly winced. Damn. How long had he been staring off into space? He was out of sorts, and his pretty companion was the reason why. Maybe Malcolm was right. Maybe he *should* start dating again. Get out there and see what the Peach State had to offer. He missed having someone special in his life, and he had no chance in hell of ever hooking up with Dionne.

Immanuel got behind the wheel of his car, started the engine and exited the parking lot. He was content driving and watching her on the sly.

"Why did you relocate to Atlanta?" Dionne said, interrupting his thoughts.

"I needed a change of scenery." He'd been asked the question dozens of times and gave everyone the same answer, but this was the first time he felt guilty about lying.

"I grew up in Italy, but I went to a university out east, so moving here wasn't much of an adjustment."

"What do you think of Atlanta so far? Do you like it?"

"So far, so good. It's a fantastic city. Southern people are incredibly charming, but there's nothing quite like living in Venice."

"I agree. I traveled to Venice last year on business, and I didn't want to come home."

"I take it you enjoyed your trip," he teased, wearing an easy smile.

"I loved everything: The food, the atmosphere, the rich architecture and history, strolling along the canals at night. It was breathtaking."

I know just how you feel, because I'm in complete and total awe of your beauty.

"Did your husband make the trip as well?"

"No." Sadness flickered across her pretty, delicate features. "The more successful I got, the more problems we had in our marriage. By the time our fifth wedding anniversary rolled around, we were living separate lives. It hurts that he couldn't support my dreams the way I championed his."

If you were my woman, I'd support you a hundred percent.

"What do you miss most about Venice?" she asked.

"My family, especially my grandparents. They helped raise me, and I owe everything I am to them. We Skype every day, but it's not the same thing as being there."

"Having Emilio nearby in Greensboro must be nice, though."

If you say so. I've never been to his estate, and I have no intention of ever visiting him.

It was a short drive to Brookhaven. Ten minutes after leaving the plaza, Immanuel pulled in front of a brick colonial-style mansion. Lush green magnolia trees surrounded the property, flower beds dotted the landscaped grounds, and the front porch held a swing and bright, comfy chairs. "This is a lot of house for one woman."

"You sound like my dad. He said I should rent a smaller place, but the bigger the better in my opinion. You only live once, right?"

"That's one way of looking at it."

"No, that's the *only* way of looking at it. I work hard. After a stressful day at the office I love nothing more than coming home to my big, beautiful mansion. Don't you?"

"You're confusing me with my brother. He's the ostentatious millionaire, not me."

"Oh, that's right. You prefer to spend your money on sports cars worth half a million."

"Who told you that?"

"Lucky guess, but you *are* driving a McLaren. They're ridiculously expensive, and I bet this is just one of many luxury cars in your collection."

"You're smart *and* clairvoyant. How fascinating."

Dionne laughed, and Immanuel did, too.

"My father and grandfather were both championship race car drivers, and I developed a love of exotic cars at a very young age," he explained. "They're my guilty pleasure."

"I'm surprised you're not a race car driver yourself."

"I couldn't cut it, but after several fits and starts I discovered my passion and built a successful business that I'm incredibly proud of."

Dionne looked impressed and nodded her head in agreement. "Good for you. As long as you're happy and doing what you love, that's all that matters."

Tell that to my father. In his eyes I'm a failure, and nothing I ever do is good enough.

Putting the car in Park, Immanuel surveyed the neighborhood, searched for anything out of the ordinary. Aside

from a woman powering up the block with her golden re-
triever, the streets were empty. Satisfied nothing was amiss,
he got out of the car and walked around to the passenger-
side door. As Dionne stood, he noticed the pained expression on her face. He could sense her anxiety and wondered
if she was reliving the attack in her mind.

"Are you okay?"

Her eyes were sad, but she nodded. "Yes, of course."

Flowers lined the walkway, perfuming the air with their
sweet, fragrant scent.

Dionne moved slowly, as if it required all of her strength,
but she flashed a thumbs-up when she caught him staring
at her. Immanuel watched her with growing admiration.
He'd never seen anyone bounce back so fast after a violent attack, and although she was sore, he knew her spirits
were strong. Dionne took her new keys out of her pocket
that he had given her at the hospital, but struggled to get
the correct one inside the lock.

"Allow me." Immanuel reached for the key ring, and
their fingers touched. It was a warm September day, a
balmy eighty degrees, but her skin was ice-cold. *She's
scared. Scared because the mugger knows where she lives.*
Anxious to get Dionne inside, he unlocked the door, pushed
it open and disabled the alarm.

The house smelled of cinnamon and vanilla. The decor
in the three-story mansion was simple but elegant. Framed
photographs, African artwork and glass sculptures decorated the foyer, giving the space a luxurious feel. Hardwood floors, indigo walls and multitiered chandeliers
dripping in crystals beautified the main floor, and the
arched windows provided natural sunlight.

"It's good to be home," she said softly, entering the gourmet kitchen. "I was only in the hospital overnight, but it
feels like weeks since I've been home."

"Are you hungry? Do you want me to make you something to eat?"

"In *my* kitchen?" Dionne laughed, as if it were the funniest thing she'd ever heard. "No thanks. I'm not hungry, just tired. I think I just need a nap."

"I don't mind sticking around until you wake up. Dr. Pelayo asked me to keep an eye on you, and I feel bad leaving you here alone."

"In *my* house?"

She sounded incredulous, looked it, too. Immanuel realized he was out of line. He wasn't her husband or family, and he had no right forcing himself on her. "I come from a large Italian family, so taking care of people is in my blood," he explained, wearing an apologetic smile. "But I'll get out of your hair and let you rest."

"Immanuel, I appreciate your concern, but I'm fine. You've done more than enough today, and you should probably go home to your family. It's almost suppertime—"

"I'm not married, and I have no children. Just a temperamental bulldog who hates me because I'm never home to play with him."

Laughing, Dionne opened the side drawer and retrieved a pen and leather-bound checkbook. "Wait a minute. I can't let you leave until I pay you." She clutched her Montblanc pen in her hand. "How much do I owe you for the clothes and cell phone?"

"Nothing. They're gifts, and I won't accept your money."

"Immanuel, that's crazy. You spent thousands of dollars on me, and I insist on paying you back."

"Thankfully, I can afford it, so please put your checkbook away."

Dionne protested, argued her case, but Immanuel wouldn't budge. He didn't want her check, not when he had more money in the bank than he could ever spend. "Italians are generous people who love spoiling their family and friends." He didn't want to offend her or come across as an obstinate jerk, so he tried to lighten the mood with a joke. "But you know who I *really* like to spoil? Strong, courageous women who fight like Jackie Chan!"

Dionne laughed, and the sound tickled his ears. A strange thing happened when their eyes met. His heart raced, and his temperature soared. His gaze zeroed in on her mouth, and the urge to kiss her was so strong, he could almost taste her lips.

"Fine, if you won't take my money, then I'll make you a hero's dinner next Friday as a token of my appreciation." Her tone brightened. "I'll make you a delicious three-course meal, and we can spend the evening getting to know each other better. I hate to brag, but my prime rib is to die for, and so is my butternut squash ravioli."

Immanuel didn't want to hurt her feelings, so he faked a smile. "That's not necessary, and furthermore I'm not a hero. *You* are."

"Your humility is endearing, but you're not fooling anyone—"

"I did what anyone in my situation would do."

"That's a lie. You bought me a designer outfit to wear home from the hospital, an iPhone 6, and a home security system. No one I've just met has ever been that benevolent."

Immanuel couldn't help but laugh. Dionne was a spitfire, a ballsy, gutsy woman with a great head on her shoulders. He found her fascinating. Few people could have done what she did last night, and the more they talked and laughed, the more he liked her.

"You're a stand-up guy, Immanuel, and now it's *my* turn to spoil *you*." Smirking, her eyes radiant and bright, she joked, "FYI, I *always* get my way. Quit while you're ahead."

Immanuel shrugged a shoulder, tried to downplay what

he'd done last night. "I have sisters, so I did what I'd want someone to do for them if they were victims of a brutal attack."

Her face fell, and the smile slid off her lips. Hanging her head, she shifted her weight from one foot to the other. "Don't say that. I fought back. I'm a survivor. Not a victim—"

Her voice cracked with emotion. Seeing her sadness, the grief that lay naked in her eyes, filled him with guilt. *I should have run faster. I should have reached her before that sick bastard knocked her to the ground.*

Immanuel moved toward her. He knew it was a mistake to touch her, but he couldn't stop himself. Her pain was profound, and he wanted to comfort her. He heard a sob escape her lips, felt her body tense, but she didn't pull away. Immanuel held her tight, close to this chest, tenderly stroking her neck and shoulders. She felt damn good in his arms, like a dream come true.

"Dionne. Dionne. Honey, where are you?"

Startled, Dionne jumped back. "It's my mom." Sniffling, she wiped her face with her hands and straightened her clothes. "I apologize in advance for what's about to happen—"

"There you are." A full-figured woman with a short Afro charged into the kitchen and wrapped Dionne in her arms. "Thank God you're all right. I was scared out of my mind."

"Mom, what's wrong? Why are you crying?" Dionne cupped her mom's face in her hands and wiped the tears from her plump brown cheeks. "Talk to me. What's the matter? When I spoke to you this morning you sounded great."

Standing in front of the French doors, Immanuel watched the exchange with growing interest. He admired the way Dionne treated her mom, how she spoke quietly to her with love and affection. And for some strange reason, seeing them embrace made Immanuel think about Emilio. *Will we ever be real brothers again?*

"I was at work, having lunch in the staff room, when I saw the story of your attack on the twelve o'clock news. I was dumbfounded, and..."

Dionne groaned in despair. For the second time in minutes tears filled her eyes. Immanuel wished he could take her back in his arms and tell her everything would be okay, but he stayed put. It wasn't his place, and he didn't want to earn the wrath of her mother. Like Dionne, her mother was petite with dark brown eyes and flawless skin. She spoke in a heavy Somali accent, and gestured wildly with her hands..

"I—I—I was on the news?" Dionne's voice was loud and panicked, thick with despair. "My clients will think I'm weak, and they'll find another coaching center—"

"The reporter didn't use your name, but I recognized your license plate number," Mrs. Osman explained. "Why didn't you say anything? Why did you lie to me?"

"Ma, I didn't want you to worry. It was nothing."

Mrs. Osman touched her cheek. "But your face is swollen, and your eyes are—"

"I'll survive. Besides, it's nothing makeup can't cover."

"I'm just glad you're okay. I don't know what I'd do if anything ever happened to you."

"Yes, you do. You'd use the insurance money to build your dream house in Somalia."

"Hush your mouth, child. Death isn't something to joke about." Mrs. Osman rested her hands on her hips and glanced around the kitchen. "Where's Jules? He should be here taking care of you. You were mugged last night, and you need him now more than ever."

Dionne groaned. "Mom, please don't do this. I'm tired.

I don't have the energy to argue with you about the sanctity of marriage and my failures as a wife."

Feeling like an intruder inside Dionne's home, Immanuel knew it was time to leave. He'd call later and apologize for leaving without saying goodbye. He turned and strode out of the kitchen, but stopped when he heard Mrs. Osman shriek. Glancing over his shoulder, he was surprised to see both women staring at him with admiration in their eyes.

"You saved my baby?"

Mrs. Osman rushed across the room and threw her arms around his shoulders. She held him so tight he feared his ribs would crack. She kissed him on each cheek, then did it again for good measure. "God bless you, young man. Thank you from the bottom of my heart."

"Ma'am, it was nothing."

Mrs. Osman furrowed her eyebrows, wearing a puzzled look. "You call saving a woman's life nothing? You're a hero, and my husband and I are forever in your debt."

Immanuel sensed it was a bad idea to argue, so he remained quiet.

"You have to join us for dinner tonight. Please, say you'll stay."

"That is very kind of you, Mrs. Osman, but I have other plans." It was a lie, but Immanuel didn't feel comfortable breaking bread with Dionne—not when his attraction to her was spiraling out of control. "All the best in your recovery. And remember what Dr. Pelayo said. Take it easy for the next few days, and don't push yourself."

"I won't, and thanks again for everything." Dionne smiled. "I'll be in touch."

Immanuel strode out of the kitchen, down the hallway and out the front door. Intent on making it downtown before the end of the business day, he hopped in his car and sped out of the cul-de-sac. In all the years he'd been working in the security business, he'd seen it all—extortion, embezzlement cases, kidnappings and even a murder attempt. After talking to Detective Sluggs that morning, he suspected someone in Dionne's inner circle was behind her attack. And the prime suspect was his new client: Jules Fontaine.

Fontaine Enterprises occupied the thirteenth floor of One Atlantic Center. The building was a national symbol of success, an iconic landmark more than three decades old. It stood fifty stories high, and was home to the most revered names in the business world. It was within walking distance of High Museum, Woodruff Arts Center, and premier restaurants, hotels and boutiques.

The lobby of Fontaine Enterprises was filled with marble and granite; everything shone and sparkled. The ten-foot windows offered unobstructed views of the city. As Immanuel approached the front desk, he straightened his navy blue Burberry tie. The receptionist, an Asian woman with fake eyelashes and peach lips, greeted him with a wide, radiant smile. "Good afternoon. Welcome to Fontaine Enterprises. How may I help you?"

"I'm Immanuel Morretti. I'm here to see Mr. Fontaine."

The receptionist opened the black leather-bound book on her desk and ran a gel nail down the right column. She narrowed her eyes and pursed her lips as if she was sucking on a lemon. "Is he expecting you?"

"Yes, of course." On the drive over, he'd called Jules several times, with no success, but the receptionist didn't need to know the truth. He had to speak to the CFO today, and he wasn't leaving Fontaine Enterprises until he did.

"I'm sorry, but Mr. Fontaine is in an important meeting and can't be disturbed."

"No problem. I'll wait."

"Very well, Mr. Morretti. Please have a seat in the waiting area." Her smile was polite, but it failed to reach her eyes. "Can I interest you in something to drink?"

Immanuel glanced over his shoulder and scanned the refreshments on the side table. "If it's not too much trouble, I'd love a cup of warm milk."

"Milk?" she repeated, wrinkling her nose.

"Yes, please, thank you."

The receptionist stood, straightened her orange A-line dress and flipped her long, silky hair over her shoulders. "Give me one moment."

"Thank you, miss. I appreciate it."

Immanuel took out his cell phone, punched in his password and scrolled through his new text messages. He pretended to be absorbed in his task, but he was watching the receptionist out of the corner of his eye. The moment she turned around, Immanuel sped through the glass doors and down the corridor. Having been to Fontaine Enterprises before, he knew exactly where to go. Confronting Jules about his suspicions could cost Immanuel his job, but he didn't care. Doing the right thing was all that mattered, and he was determined to uncover the truth.

At the end of the hall, Immanuel turned left and stopped at the corner office. He knocked on the door, then threw it open. A woman with big hair and fuchsia lips hopped to her feet and fussed with her clothes. Jules sat behind his executive desk, wearing a sly, dirty grin.

"Immanuel, what are you doing here?" Jules spoke to Immanuel, but his gaze remained glued to the brunette's ass. "I'm busy."

"I need to talk to you about Dionne. It's important."

Jules gave a curt nod, rudely dismissing the brunette with a flick of his hands.

The mystery woman fled the office and closed the door behind her. A modern mix of leather, wood and glass, the space was an extravagant display of luxury and wealth.

Certificates and awards were prominently displayed on the mounted wall shelves, but Immanuel wasn't impressed. Born into a rich family, Jules Fontaine had had everything handed to him, though he foolishly believed *he* was the reason for his success. He was a loud, opinionated prick, and if not for his charity work and million-dollar donations, Immanuel would think the man had no heart.

"I don't have time to shoot the breeze, so make this quick."

Of course you don't. You're too busy getting blow jobs from your female staff. There was something about Jules Fontaine that irked him, that set his teeth on edge. He carried himself in a smug manner, as if he owned the world and everyone in it. Immanuel couldn't figure out how Jules—a short, average-looking guy—had scored a woman like Dionne. Immanuel suspected the businessman had showered her with expensive gifts to win her heart.

"Dionne was robbed last night."

He shrugged and leaned back in his chair. "What does that have to do with me?"

"Don't you care?"

"No. She's been acting like a spoiled brat for months, and I've had enough. Hopefully, this assault will knock some sense into her, *literally.*" Reclining in his chair, as if he was tanning on the beach, he clasped his hands behind his head and propped his legs up on his desk. "Her attack could turn out to be a blessing in disguise."

Immanuel's eyes thinned, and his body shook with uncontrollable rage. He felt his hands curl into fists and imagined himself punching Jules in the face. He hated men who mistreated women, and stared at the businessman with disdain.

Jules must have sensed what was coming, must have seen the murderous expression on Immanuel's face, because he now wore an apologetic smile. "Forgive me. That came out wrong. What I meant to say was that I hope this experience reminds Dionne how precious life is. I'm her husband, and I deserve to be treated with gratitude and respect."

"Did you have anything to do with the assault? Did you hire that creep to rough her up?"

"What are you, a cop now? I don't answer to you. Now, get out of my office, and don't come back until you have evidence of Dionne's infidelity." A grin claimed his lips. "And I don't care what you have to do to get it—even if you have to set her up."

A chill whipped through Immanuel's body. Everything became clear. Why Jules had hired him. Why he'd insisted he personally handle this case. His experience working on high-profile cases had nothing to do with it. Jules knew about the scandal in Venice—the one that had destroyed his business and his reputation—and thought he could manipulate him into doing something shady to frame Dionne. It was obvious Jules was a jerk, a snake of the lowest kind, and Immanuel wanted no part of his sick, devious plot. "I quit."

"You can't quit. We have a contract."

"Just watch me."

The men stared each other down, glaring at each other with contempt.

"I think you had something to do with Dionne's attack, and since I don't do business with criminals, our contract is null and void, effective immediately."

"If you screw me over, I'll run your business into the ground."

Immanuel turned and walked back through the office. He knew he was doing the right thing, making a wise decision, and there was nothing Jules could say to change his mind. "I don't give a damn what you do. I don't respect men who abuse women."

"I hired you for a reason, and I expect you to do your job."

Stopping, he wheeled around and faced Jules once again. "I'm going to ask you one more time, and this time I want the truth. Did you hire someone to hurt your estranged wife?"

"Of course not. I'd never do anything to hurt her. She's my life, my everything..."

Sure she is. That's why you're screwing other women.

"I need you to watch out for her," he continued. "Dionne has a lot of enemies, and—"

"Really?" Immanuel cocked an eyebrow. "Like who?"

"Dionne isn't the easiest person to work for, and over the years several of her employees have threatened her. Most recently, Brad McClendon."

A sour taste filled his mouth. Someone had threatened Dionne? Why didn't she tell the police? Why was she protecting her ex-employee? Were they lovers?

"Imagine how you'd feel if Dionne got hurt again and you weren't there to protect her."

That's my biggest fear.

"Stay on the case. I'll double your salary."

Immanuel was troubled, unsure of what to do. He sensed Jules was lying to him, saying what he thought he wanted to hear. It was apparent someone was after Dionne. He needed sound advice and knew who to call. "I'll be in touch."

Immanuel then turned and marched out of the office. As he strode down the corridor, his doubts intensified. He couldn't shake the feeling that Jules was playing him, and that was reason enough to stay away from the smug CFO. A meeting with his attorney was definitely in order, because the sooner Immanuel severed ties with Jules Fontaine, the better.

Chapter 6

Dionne loved Mel and Lorna and appreciated their taking time out of their busy day to visit her, but she wanted her sisters out of her house, now. They'd overstayed their welcome, and their incessant questions about the attack and Jules's whereabouts had her on edge. She woke up that morning with the intention of going to the office, but when she looked in the mirror and saw her puffy eyes and swollen face, she decided to work from home. Just as she'd entered her home office, her sisters had arrived with breakfast. As they sat down in the kitchen to eat, Sharleen had shown up with flowers and get-well balloons. Upon learning about Dionne's attack, she'd cut her romantic trip short and promptly returned to Atlanta. Dionne appreciated the sacrifices she'd made and thanked her for being a terrific friend and vice president.

The women sat at the kitchen table, eating and chatting, but Dionne wasn't hungry. Nor was she interested in joining the conversation. It was a challenge to stay awake when all she wanted to do was curl up on the couch and sleep.

Dionne yawned and stretched her sore, achy arms in the air. Tossing and turning all night, she'd had horrible dreams about the attack, nightmares so frightening she was scared to fall asleep. Dionne was nervous about leaving the house, afraid the mugger was outside lurking in the shadows. She wished Immanuel were there to protect her.

Thinking about her real-life hero—the man who'd risked his life to save hers—brought a smile to her lips. What struck her most about Immanuel, besides his good looks, was his kindness and generosity. That's why Dionne wanted to see him again, to return the favor. He'd turned her down twice, but she wasn't giving up. She wanted to do something special for Immanuel, and considered asking Sharleen for advice.

"Dionne, Mom's right." Mel reached for her glass of orange juice and took a drink. "Jules *should* be here with you. He's your husband, and you need him now more than ever."

No, what I need is for you to get off my back.

Mel was a wife and a mother of two, with caramel skin, a slender shape and ridiculously long legs. When she wasn't chasing after her toddler sons, she was doing yoga, whipping up vegan recipes and caring for her elderly mother-in-law.

"You were mugged, and that crook knows where you live." Lorna shivered, as if chilled to the bone. "You shouldn't be by yourself at a time like this. You should be with Jules, in your marital home, not going it alone here in Brookhaven. "

Dionne didn't want to talk about the attack, and she damn sure didn't want to talk about her marriage. Why couldn't her sisters understand that? Why were they being so judgmental? And why were they pushing her to reconcile with Jules? He'd called last night, supposedly to check up on her, but spent the entire conversation talking about himself. He'd been nominated for Atlanta Businessperson of the Year, and wanted her to accompany him to the award luncheon in November. As if. The event was just days before their court date, and Dionne would rather swim with sharks than pretend to be his dutiful wife.

"Jules is a good man, and if I were you I'd reconcile with him before it's too late."

Is she high? Dionne didn't want to argue. Her sisters didn't know what it was like to be in a loveless marriage, and she resented their telling her what to do, especially Lorna. The Atlanta housewife was married to a celebrity manager, the mother of three teenagers and bossy as hell. But Dionne wasn't having it. Not today. She had a mind of her own, a strong sense of self, and she wasn't taking Lorna's stupid advice. "I appreciate your concern, but my marriage is none of your business. You don't know what it was like living with Jules—"

"Dionne, spare me," Mel snapped. "I've been married twice as long as you have, and I've never once left my husband. We make it work, no matter what."

"That's easy for you to say. Francisco is a great husband and father. He'd never dream of stepping out on you. He's loyal and trustworthy. It's obvious he loves you very much."

Lorna reached across the table and patted Dionne's hand. "I'll ask Randle to speak to Jules on your behalf. They get along great, and I'm sure my husband can talk some sense into him. You'll see. You guys will be back together in no time."

"Please don't," Dionne said, shaking her head. "It'll only make things worse, and Jules will be pissed that I told you about his affairs."

Sharleen gasped. "Affairs? As in more than one? Why didn't you say anything?"

"So, Jules is sowing his wild oats." Lorna twirled an

index finger in the air and gave a dismissive shrug of her shoulders. "Big deal. Cheating is not a deal breaker."

"It's not?" Dionne and Sharleen shouted in unison.

"Not to me. As long as my husband pays the bills, respects my role as his wife and gives me a healthy weekly allowance, I don't give a damn what he does in his free time."

Stunned, Dionne couldn't speak. *What is this, the Dark Ages? Doesn't she realize how insecure she sounds?* She studied Lorna's face, searching her eyes for clues. *She's just trying to get a rise out of me, right?* Their mother had raised them to be strong, independent women, and Lorna's views about love and relationships went against everything they'd been taught.

"You know what your problem is, Dionne? You let success go to your head."

Her body tensed and anger pounded furiously through her veins. "Are you saying it's *my* fault that Jules cheated on me?" she roared. "Are you blaming me for *his* mistakes?"

"I'm not condoning what Jules did, but he's not entirely to blame for the problems in your marriage. You modern, career-driven types don't know the first thing about the opposite sex, and you've deluded yourself into thinking you don't need a man, but you do."

Sharleen dropped her fork on her plate and hitched a hand to her hip. "I disagree."

Mel snickered. "Of course you do. You're as misguided as Dionne is."

"I *can* have it all. A career I love, the man of my dreams *and* children if I choose," she said, her tone filled with pride. "Emilio added to my life, but he's not my whole life. I adore him but I had goals and ambitions long before I ever met him, and I plan to fulfill each and every one."

"You're deceiving yourself if you think you can have it all, because you can't."

"How would *you* know?" Dionne shot back. It was her life, and she wasn't going to let her sisters bully her into reconciling with Jules. He'd broken her spirit every time he lied to her, and Dionne was tired of pretending they were living the American dream. Their marriage couldn't be saved, and if Lorna didn't like that, it was too damn bad. "You got married straight out of high school, and you've never worked outside of the home."

Her gaze was dark with venom. "This isn't about me. This is about *your* failed marriages."

"Marriage is hard work, and you can't quit at the first sign of trouble."

"The first sign of trouble?" Dionne repeated, raising her voice. "Mel, don't you *dare* call me a quitter. You don't know what it's like to go to bed every night and not know where your husband is. Jules doesn't want a wife, he wants a puppet, and I can't take it anymore."

"And you shouldn't have to. No one should." Sharleen wore a sympathetic smile, but her eyes glimmered with mischief. "Cheating is a deal breaker to me, so I commend you for taking the high road. I would've doused car with gasoline and lit a match."

For the first time in days, Dionne laughed. Laughed so hard water filled her eyes. Her sisters stared at her as if she were out of her mind, but Dionne didn't care. Joking around with Sharleen made her feel good, less scared and stressed out. Her friend was a positive, optimistic soul, and her words of encouragement bolstered her spirits.

"You have to do what's right for you and *only* you."

"Thanks, girl. I really needed to hear that."

"All great changes are preceded by chaos, and I suspect this is going to be a banner year for you," Sharleen said with a wink. "Hang in there, boss. Things will get better. I know it."

"If you divorce Jules you'll live to regret it."

No one asked you, so mind your own business.

"Adeline called me last night, and we spoke at length about your marital problems," Lorna said in a somber tone, as if she were delivering a eulogy at a funeral. "She's very upset about the separation, and so are her parents."

Of course they are. They act like they're perfect, but they're not. They have flaws, insecurities and fears just like the rest of us.

"Go back home," Mel urged. "It's the right thing to do for everyone involved—"

Hearing her cell phone ring, Dionne excused herself from the table and grabbed her iPhone off the breakfast bar. The conversation was getting too heavy for her, giving her an excruciating headache, and she feared she'd soon say something she'd regret.

As Dionne exited the kitchen, she overheard Sharleen ask Mel about her wedding day. Her vice president was charming, and when Dionne heard her sisters giggle she knew they were eating out of her friend's palm.

The screen said "unknown number," but since it could be a prospective client calling to book a free consultation, Dionne took the call and spoke in a bright, confident voice. "Hello, Dionne Fontaine speaking."

Click. Dionne hung up the phone, and it rang almost immediately again. Same result. Annoyed, she wondered if there was something she could do about it. She made a mental note to ask Detective Sluggs the next time they spoke. All morning, she'd received prank calls, and it was getting on her nerves. It was probably Jules, trying to scare her. Dionne wasn't going to let him intimidate her or pressure her into returning to their marital home. She had everything going for her, and she wasn't going to let her ex call the shots anymore. It was time to stand on her own two feet, and—

Her cell phone rang yet again. Dionne froze, but when she saw the name on the screen, her spirits soared. She cleared her throat and answered on the second ring. "Hello."

"Good morning, Dionne. It's Immanuel Morretti."

A smile bloomed in her heart and spread to her lips. *That* voice. That dreamy, husky voice excited her every time. Her thoughts returned to Thursday afternoon, to the exact moment Immanuel had taken her into his arms and held her close. It was seared into her memory, and for as long as she lived she'd never forget how safe he made her feel. "It's good to hear from you," she said quietly, meaning every word.

"How are you feeling?"

"Terrific. As long as I have wine and chocolate nothing can *ever* get me down."

Immanuel chuckled. "That's valuable information. I'll have to remember that."

For a moment, Dionne forgot about her troubles—the attack, her impending court date, the argument with her sisters minutes earlier—and enjoyed her conversation with Immanuel. He was easy to talk to, a calm, quiet soul, and she appreciated his calling to check on her.

"Have you had breakfast?" he asked. "I'm at the Waffle House near the Brookhaven shopping center, and I thought you might want something to eat."

"That's very sweet of you, Immanuel, but I already ate."

Laughter exploded inside the kitchen, floating down the hall and into the living room. Dionne wondered what her sisters and Sharleen were cackling about, then moved toward the bay window so Immanuel wouldn't hear their boisterous laughter.

"You have company."

"Yes, Sharleen and my sisters came by with breakfast, but they're leaving shortly..." *So if you want to come by for a visit, that would be great.* Dionne wanted to see Immanuel again, but couldn't bring herself to invite him over for lunch. She wasn't used to making the first move, and didn't want him to think she was desperate.

"My apologies for interrupting. I'll let you return to your guests."

Disappointment filled her, but she pushed back her emotions. Immanuel had called to check up on her, which meant he cared about her, right? Feeling hopeful, she expelled a nervous breath and spoke with confidence. "Do you have plans next Sunday? I'd love to have you over for brunch. Or we can meet somewhere in town if you'd like. My treat."

Silence infected the line, and seconds ticked by on the clock hanging above her couch.

"I'm sorry, I can't. I have to work."

"I understand. Maybe next time."

"Take care of yourself, Dionne. Get plenty of rest and drink a lot of fluids," he advised. "It takes several days to recover from a concussion, so don't push yourself too hard."

"You sound like Dr. Pelayo," she joked, hoping to make him laugh.

He did, and her heart swelled with pride. Dionne felt like a teenager again—giddy, self-conscious and nervous—and Immanuel Morretti was the reason. His old-fashioned ways were endearing, and so was his Italian accent. He was the polar opposite of her ex, but that was a plus. Dionne was curious about him, wanted to get to know him better. *What does he do for fun? What are his hobbies and interests? Is he dating anyone?*

"Dr. Pelayo knows her stuff. You should listen to her."

Her spirits sank, and her shoulders drooped. Is that why

he didn't want to come over? Because he was interested in the pretty doctor?

"Bye, Dionne."

She nodded and swallowed the lump in her throat. "Bye, Immanuel. Thanks for calling."

The line went dead, and she slumped against the bay window with a heavy heart. It was times like this Dionne wished her brother, Kwame, were around. They had a strong bond, always had, and every time he called from Melbourne they talked and laughed for hours. He was a forty-year-old web designer, working abroad in Australia, and Dionne missed him dearly. Unlike her sisters, he was supportive and sympathetic and gave great advice.

"Dionne, I have to run."

"Me, too," Mel said. "The boys have a soccer game at noon, and I promised I'd be there."

Breaking free of her thoughts, Dionne followed her sisters to the front door. She could tell by their tight smiles that they were mad at her, but Dionne didn't care. She'd done nothing wrong and wasn't going to apologize for having a mind of her own.

"Kiss the kids for me and tell them Auntie loves them very much."

As her sisters got in Lorna's shiny white convertible, Dionne waved. They drove her nuts sometimes, but they were her family, and she couldn't imagine life without them. Hopefully, Mel and Lorna would be in a better mood the next time they spoke, because the last thing Dionne wanted was for her sisters to be mad at her. *I have enough on my plate as it is.*

Standing on the porch, she felt the sun on her face, the light autumn breeze. There wasn't a cloud in sight, nothing but clear blue skies for as far as her eyes could see.

Glancing up and down the block, Dionne searched for anything suspicious. *Is the mugger nearby? Is he watching me right now? Plotting his next move?* At the terrifying thought, perspiration drenched her skin in a cold sweat. Dionne focused her gaze, giving her property a thorough search. Finding nothing, she sighed in relief. Later, after her nap, she'd call the police and get an update on the case. Not knowing what was going on was nerve-racking.

Dionne returned to the kitchen and found Sharleen standing outside on the patio deck, talking on her cell phone in Italian. She'd been taking Italian language classes for months and enjoyed practicing with Emilio. Dionne guessed Sharleen was making plans with him, something wonderfully romantic. They were always calling and texting each other, and when her vice president wasn't at the office, she was out and about with Emilio. Dionne was thrilled for Sharleen, glad her friend had found a loving, supportive man who treated her like a queen.

I didn't, but I have no one to blame but myself.

"You should go in the living room and rest." Sharleen closed the patio door, joined Dionne at the kitchen sink and took the soap sponge from her hands. "I can finish up in here."

"Let's do it together. We can brainstorm new ad campaigns while we clean."

Sharleen beamed. "*Or*, we can talk about my Venice wedding."

Sharleen talked, and Dionne listened. She had questions about Immanuel—lots and lots of questions—but since she didn't want to give her friend the wrong impression, she wisely kept her thoughts to herself. "How did you find out about the attack?" Dionne asked, curious.

"Annabelle saw the story on the evening news and called me right away."

Why am I not surprised? "Juicy gossip" should be her middle name.

"You're the heart and soul of Pathways Center, so I'm glad that you're okay."

"Thanks, Sharleen. Me, too."

"Will you be in tomorrow?" Sharleen asked, returning the cleaning supplies to the closet.

"I'm going to work from home this week, but I'll definitely be in Friday."

Sharleen cheered. "Good, so we can head straight to the spa after work. I could use a hot stone massage, and I bet you could, too."

"You can say that again. It's been a hell of a week, and I can use a bit of pampering."

"I hear you. Planning a wedding in a foreign country for 250 guests is stressful. If Emilio invites one more person I quit, and we're eloping to Vegas."

Dionne cracked up, laughed out loud when her friend made a silly face.

"Do you like baseball?" Sharleen asked, sliding her cell phone into her back pocket. "Emilio's cousin Demetri plays for the Chicago Royals, and he invited us to watch his World Series game from his private luxury box. It's on the twenty-ninth. What do you say?"

Dionne opened the fridge and grabbed the bottle of juice. "I better not," she said, filling two glasses. "I know nothing about baseball, and I don't want to embarrass myself."

"You have to come. There'll be terrific food, an open bar, and plenty of opportunities to network with influential people and wealthy baseball executives."

"Why didn't you say that sooner? Networking is my specialty," Dionne said with a laugh. "Count me in. I'd love to go."

The women clinked glasses and shared a smile.

"Will Immanuel be there?"

Sharleen raised an eyebrow. "I don't know. Why? Do you like him?"

"Of course not. I'm just curious, that's all."

"I still can't believe he rescued you from that deranged mugger on Thursday. Crazy, huh?"

You can say that again, Dionne thought, exiting the kitchen. *Even crazier? I can't stop thinking about him, and last night I dreamed he kissed me.*

Dionne entered the living room and flopped down on the couch.

"I can't wait to meet Immanuel. What's he like?"

He's wordly, sophisticated and hot, Dionne thought. Taking a deep breath to calm her raging heartbeat, she opened up to Sharleen about the attack, her hospital stay, and all the kind and thoughtful things Immanuel had done for her. "I offered to write him a check when he brought me home on Friday, but he refused."

"I'm not surprised. He's a multimillionaire. He doesn't need your money."

Dionne felt her eyes widen and her jaw drop. "A multimillionaire? Wow, who knew the security business was so profitable? Girl, we should buy shares in Mastermind Operations."

Sharleen cracked up. "I know, huh? Emilio and Immanuel's brother, Dante, is a real estate developer, and he had encouraged them to invest in the real estate market. Emilio says it's the smartest decision he's ever made." She added, "Besides proposing to me, of course."

"Okay, I get it, Immanuel doesn't need my money, but I'd still like to do something special for him," she said. "Every time I invite him over he turns me down, and it's frustrating."

"Then kidnap him. Once he's your hostage you can have your way with him."

Dionne laughed, but an idea sparked in her mind. Excitement warmed her skin, and goose bumps exploded across her chest. Dionne knew just what to do to thank Immanuel—her tall, dark and handsome hero—and couldn't wait to see the look on his face when she surprised him. She'd need a few days to arrange everything, but she was confident her plan would work. "Sharleen, you're amazing," she praised, leaning over and giving her friend a one-arm hug. "You just helped solve my problem."

"I did?" she asked, surprise coloring her cheeks. "What are you going to do?"

Dionne smirked. "Girl, if I tell you, I'd have to kill you!"

Chapter 7

Immanuel was supposed to be working. He had emails to answer, cases to review and memos to write, but he couldn't stop thinking about Dionne. He wondered if going to the gym would help take his mind off the fearless lady with the effervescent personality—

No, argued his inner voice. *You'll just obsess about her while you're at Sampson's Gym.*

His gaze landed on the wall clock hanging above his office door, and his eyes narrowed. Every day at six o'clock, he called Dionne to check in with her. Their conversations were brief, only a few minutes, but he looked forward to hearing her voice at the end of the day. It had been a week since the attack, and every day she sounded stronger and more upbeat. He'd called her cell phone twice, but with no luck. The suspense was killing him, driving him insane. Dionne wasn't his girlfriend and he had no claims on her, but he hated not being able to reach her. He felt in his gut that something was wrong and considered going to her home to check on her. *After all, we're neighbors*, he reasoned. *That's what neighbors do. They look out for each other.*

Immanuel picked up his desk phone, but he didn't hit Redial. Something held him back, preventing him from dialing. It was his attraction to Dionne, the white-hot chemistry they shared. He was playing with fire, and feared if he wasn't careful he'd end up doing something he regretted—like kissing her passionately the next time he saw her.

Dropping the phone in the cradle, he picked up the manila envelope beside the pendant lamp. The package had arrived that morning via UPS, but Immanuel still hadn't decided whether or not he was going to Demetri's game. He loved baseball and didn't have any plans that particular night, but he didn't want to go to the stadium alone. If his sister were in town she'd go to the game with him, but Francesca was in Italy visiting relatives and wouldn't be back in Atlanta until after Emilio's wedding. Immanuel thought of inviting Malcolm, but the last time they attended a sporting event together, his friend had ditched him for a voluptuous redhead and hadn't resurfaced until the end of the game.

His thoughts wandered, returning to the woman who'd starred in his dreams last night. *Does Dionne like baseball? Should I invite her to the game?* Demetri's luxury suite would be filled with friends, family and associates, and Immanuel wanted to have someone to enjoy the game with— someone witty and fun. He knew only one woman who fit the bill.

Staring out the window, Immanuel leaned back in his leather executive chair. His mind returned to last Friday, and images of Dionne filled his mind. On the drive from the Atlanta Medical Center to Brookhaven they'd talked with ease, as if they'd known each other for years, rather than a few hours. He appreciated Dionne's candor, found her honesty refreshing. Immanuel didn't have any female friends and liked hearing Dionne's take on relationships, business and pop culture.

"Man, you're a pitiful sight…"

Immanuel blinked, spotting his business partner, Malcolm Black, standing in the doorway, and straightened in his chair. He scooped up his pen and made notes on the document sitting on the middle of his desk, pretending to be hard at work. "I'm just taking a short break," he said, feeling the need to defend himself. "It's been crazy busy around here, but I've made a ton of progress on the online marketing campaign—"

"Busy my ass. You haven't done jack shit all day, and you know it."

Malcolm closed the door, marched into the office and plopped down on the edge of Immanuel's L-shaped mahogany desk.

"Man, is everything okay? You've been acting strange."

"I'm good. Couldn't be better."

"Liar! Either you're in love or you're having a nervous breakdown. Which one is it?"

Immanuel gave a hearty laugh. "None of the above."

"Good. Just checking." Malcolm turned serious, wore a pensive expression on his face. He spoke openly about staff concerns, his goals for the agency and security practices he wanted to implement for high-profile clients.

Immanuel lost his focus. He glanced discreetly at his watch, saw that it was six thirty, and decided to call it a day. No use staying at the office. His thoughts were on Dionne, and he wouldn't be able to get anything done until he heard from her.

"Mr. Fontaine made a second payment today," Malcolm said. "And it was five figures."

Immanuel groaned. Damn. That's the last thing he wanted to hear.

"I called his office to alert him of the error, but his secretary said you'd know what the additional payment was for. Fill me in."

The case was confidential, deeply personal, and Immanuel didn't feel comfortable discussing it with Malcolm. His partner sucked at paperwork and couldn't write a memo to save his life, but he was the heart and soul of the agency. Efficiency improved once the former navy SEAL took over the HR department. Everyone on staff loved Malcolm's gregarious personality. If he told his friend about his feelings for Dionne—that he was romantically interested in her—the whole office would know by the end of the week.

"Does the additional payment have something to do with Mrs. Fontaine's brutal attack?"

Needing a moment to think, Immanuel nodded absently. Annoyed at himself for not standing his ground last Friday at Fontaine Enterprises, he plotted his next move. Jules had him backed into a corner and had effectively bought his silence by issuing a second payment. Even though Immanuel suspected Jules had something to do with Dionne's attack, he couldn't prove it, and if he pissed off the CFO it could cost him his career. *I'm too old to start over again. Mastermind Operations Atlanta* has *to work. This is my last chance.*

"Mr. Fontaine is worried about his estranged wife and wants additional security for her."

"That's odd. Most divorcés pay to kill their spouses, not keep them alive." Malcolm exploded in laughter as if his joke were the funniest thing he'd ever heard. "I heard Mrs. Fontaine is a battle-ax, so I'm not surprised she has enemies."

"Who told you that?"

"One of her female life coaches. I met Annabelle a few weeks ago at Sampson's Gym, and she had nothing nice to say about her boss."

Was Annabelle the disgruntled employee out to get Dionne?

"That's not my perception of her at all. To be honest, she's one of the most fascinating, interesting women I've ever met and I've worked with some of the biggest stars in the world."

"It sounds like *someone* has a crush on Mr. Fontaine's wife."

"I'm just calling it as I see it," Immanuel said with a shrug. "Sometimes being the boss sucks. I know firsthand how stressful it is to man a successful company. You don't know who to trust, and your employees will stab you in the back without a second thought."

"This isn't Venice, Immanuel. What happened in Italy isn't going to happen here."

I sure hope not.

"I look forward to meeting Mrs. Fontaine. I heard she has a lot of celebrity clients. Befriending her could be great for Mastermind Operations."

"I think you're going to like her. She's strong, fearless and successful in her own right."

And did I mention she's ridiculously beautiful, too?

"Then assign *me* to her case, because I could use a sugar mama."

An idea suddenly came to Immanuel. It was the answer to all of his problems. He'd give Jules exactly what he wanted. He'd assign his best employee to Dionne's case to follow her until her attacker was caught. He felt a dull ache in his chest, a familiar pain. Immanuel hadn't done anything wrong; he was just doing his job, but his guilt was tremendous. *Should I tell Dionne the truth? Will she understand, or lash out at me in anger?*

"Let's split the money in half, right down the middle." Wearing an intense face, Malcolm hopped to his feet and pleaded his case with conviction. "I could use a new set of wheels."

"Another one? But you just bought a classic Mustang last week."

"A man can never have too many toys." He added with a sly grin, "Or women."

Immanuel turned off his computer. He had to get going. Anxious to see Dionne, he picked up his car keys off the desk and stood. As he grabbed his suit jacket off the back of his chair, he caught sight of his reflection in the wall mirror. He hated the scar along his jaw, hated the man who'd put it there even more. Every time he thought about that fateful night, anger consumed him. Casting aside the bitter memory, he swallowed hard. "I'm heading out now. Do you mind locking up?"

Malcolm whistled, made a show of looking at his diamond wristwatch. "This is a first. You must have somewhere important to be because you never leave the office before sunset."

His partner was fishing for information, but since telling him about his plans would inevitably come back to haunt him, Immanuel changed the subject. He loved Malcolm like a brother and couldn't have asked for a better business partner, but he didn't want anyone to know his feelings for Dionne, especially not the office gossip. "What are you getting into tonight?"

"You mean *besides* the Brunson twins?" Malcolm popped the collar on his navy blue dress shirt. "They practically begged me to come over tonight..."

Immanuel stood there listening to his business partner brag about his sexual conquest and felt a mixture of pity and disgust. *Will I turn out to be just like Malcolm one day? Is this what I want? To be a forty-five-year-old bachelor with no wife, no kids and no future?* Immanuel would never admit it to anyone, but he was jealous of his cousins. By all accounts, Demetri, Nicco and Rafael were living the American dream. Hell, so was Emilio. They had fantastic careers, success and most important, the love of good women. *What do I have?*

A big house and no one to share it with, that's what, answered his inner voice.

As Immanuel exited his office with Malcolm in tow, he thought about the last conversation he'd had with his grandmother, Gianna. He heard her soft, soothing voice playing in his mind as he stalked down the dimly lit corridor.

I'm not getting any younger, mio figlio, *and neither are you. I want to see you get married before I die. Is that too much to ask?*

Moved by her heartfelt plea, he'd promised to do as she asked, to look for a suitable bride, but he was no closer to settling down than Malcolm was. The past three years had been plagued with highs and lows—more lows than he cared to admit—but Immanuel was through feeling sorry for himself. His fiancée was long gone, and she wasn't coming back. It was time to move on, to find his soul mate and bring her home to his beloved grandmother. *I wish I could meet someone like Dionne,* he thought.

No, you don't, argued his inner voice. *You wish you could have her for yourself.*

The reception area was deserted, and the air held the faint scent of coffee. His stomach groaned, releasing a torrent of rumbles, but food was the last thing on Immanuel's mind. He was worried about Dionne, afraid that she'd met ill will, and—

A blinding light flashed in the reception area, drawing Immanuel's gaze across the room. A white limousine with tinted windows stopped at the curb, and the driver jumped out. He marched briskly around the car, opened the passenger door and stepped aside.

Immanuel hung his head. *Damn. What is Mr. Fontaine doing here?* The CFO had arrived at Mastermind Operations in a limo weeks earlier. *What does he want now? Hasn't he done enough? Why won't he back off, and let me do my job?*

"Looks like you have a visitor." Malcolm clapped a hand on Immanuel's shoulder and gestured to the corridor with a flick of his head. "Go out the back. I'll get rid of him."

Shaking his head, he masked his frustration with a smile. Mastermind Operations was his life, his brainchild, and he wasn't going to shirk his responsibilities because he disliked his newest client. But once he got rid of the cocky CFO, he was going to find Dionne. "Don't worry. I got this. I can handle Jules Fontaine."

Immanuel stuffed his keys into his pocket and buttoned up his suit jacket. He was quickly glancing around the reception area, ensuring everything was in order, when he heard Malcolm gasp. "Lord have mercy. Feet don't fail me now."

Immanuel looked up just in time to see Dionne emerge from the backseat of the limousine. She straightened to her full height, ran her hands along the side of her black couture gown, and glided—not walked—down the sidewalk. It was a dress intended to turn heads, and it did. Everyone on the street stopped and stared.

Time slowed, crawled to a stop. For the first time in Immanuel's life he was speechless, couldn't do anything but stare. He felt a mixture of apprehension and relief. He was glad that Dionne was okay, but the sight of her dressed to kill in a figure-hugging lace dress and knee-high leather boots took his breath away.

His eyes appraised her look, admiring every aspect of her appearance—the side ponytail, the dramatic makeup, the gold teardrop earrings that grazed her shoulders. Immanuel liked the cut of her dress, liked how it skimmed her curves and hips.

"Who is *that*?" Malcolm asked, licking his lips. "And where has she been all my life?"

"That's Dionne Fontaine."

His jaw dropped, and his eyes widened. Seconds passed before Malcolm spoke, and when he did, his voice was filled with awe. "How did Jules score a honey like that?"

Your guess is as good as mine. He doesn't deserve her. Never has, never will.

"It's an open secret that Jules cheats on her, but why? If that were my wife I'd burn my little black book, quit my job and work from home."

That makes two of us. I'd probably never leave the house again.

"Damn, she's coming this way." Malcolm raked a hand through his hair and straightened his burgundy dress shirt. "How do I look? Are my clothes okay? Do you think she'll like me?"

Immanuel chuckled, couldn't help it. His partner was losing it. Unfortunately, he knew how Malcolm felt. Dionne had that effect on him, too, and it took every ounce of his self-control not to crush his lips against her mouth every single time she smiled at him.

Dionne entered the office, moved toward him with deliberate intent. She had a lovely face and sexy lips, and her walk was mesmerizing. She always looked like a star, as if she were at a red carpet event. Tonight was no exception. Everything about Dionne's appearance excited him, made him want to kiss and stroke her.

Immanuel wiped his brow with the back of his hand. He was sweating, burning up in his tailored suit, and his throat was bone-dry. Her fruity perfume filled the air, tickled and teased his nostrils. The scent made him hanker for a cold glass of strawberry lemonade.

Her eyes were on him, watching him, appraising him, and Immanuel wondered what she was thinking. Dionne waved, blessed him with a smile, and his brain turned to mush. He couldn't think, couldn't speak, felt his pulse beating erratically.

Taking a deep breath helped Immanuel gather himself. He was a grown-ass man, a Morretti no less, and nothing could rattle him   not even a seductive woman with curves like a winding road—so he nodded politely at Dionne and slid his hands into his pocket.

Feeling confident and back in control, Immanuel stepped forward and offered his right hand in greeting. Dionne pretended it wasn't there and touched his forearm. His heart lurched, froze inside the walls of his chest, and his flesh quivered with uncontrollable need. Dionne leaned in, pressed herself flat against him, and kissed him on each cheek.

Desire singed Immanuel's skin, set his body ablaze. Her smile was dazzling, so bright it could light up the city center, and if they were alone he would've returned the gesture, kissed her hard, passionately, with fire and desire. He craved her, longed to have her in his arms and in his bed. His feelings for her were insatiable, out of control. But since Immanuel would never do anything to compromise his reputation, he tore his gaze away from her mouth and stepped back.

"Wow, Immanuel, you look amazing," she gushed. "Very dashing and debonair."

Malcolm cleared his throat and stepped forward. "I'm Malcolm Black, co-owner of Mastermind Operations," he said with a wide, toothy grin. "Welcome to the agency, Mrs. Fontaine. To what do we owe this pleasure?"

"I'm taking your partner out for dinner tonight."

Malcolm cocked an eyebrow. "Is that right? Funny, he never mentioned it."

"That's because it's a surprise."

"Sounds intriguing," Malcolm said, stroking his jaw. "Tell me more."

But she didn't. Dionne turned to Immanuel and gave him her undivided attention. Her gaze was on him, glued to his face, and she spoke in a reverent tone of voice. "This is my way of saying thank you for everything you've done for me."

"You've expressed your gratitude several times—"

"I know, but I want to do something *extra* special for you." Her eyes shimmered with excitement, and a smile warmed her moist red lips. "You have to eat, and I have to eat, so we might as well do it together. Shall we?"

"It doesn't look like I have much of a choice."

"That's because you don't."

Immanuel wanted to protest, but when Dionne winked at him he forgot what he was going to say. She was trying to impress him, to prove she had deep pockets, but it wasn't necessary. There was nothing sexier than confidence, and she was swimming in it. That's what intrigued him about her.

"Let's go. We have a fabulous night ahead of us, one you won't soon forget." The matter decided, she stepped forward and looped an arm through his. Dionne led him through the building, out the front door and to the waiting car.

The limousine driver bowed chivalrously at the waist, then opened the passenger door.

"Do you always drive around town in a limo?" Immanuel asked, cocking an eyebrow.

"I wish. My car's still MIA, so I decided to rent something fancy for our date..."

Our date? Her words echoed in his mind. *Is that what this is? A date?* A grin claimed his mouth. Immanuel hadn't been out in months. Not since his disastrous double date with Malcolm and the Brunson twins, and he liked the idea of spending some time alone with Dionne. "Do the police have any suspects in custody?"

"No, unfortunately they don't. I spoke to detectives this morning, and they assured me they're working hard on the case, but I've lost all hope of them ever finding my Lexus. It's probably been stripped of its parts and sold to a chop shop by now."

"Stripped of its parts and sold to a chop shop? Where did you learn to talk like that?"

"I watch TV. I know what's up." Dionne climbed inside the limousine, crossed her legs, and patted the seat beside her. "Get in. You can tell me about your day on the way to the restaurant, and if you play your cards right I just might give you a glass of Cristal."

"Where are we going?"

"It's a surprise."

Chuckling, Immanuel ducked inside the car.

Chapter 8

Bacchanalia, the most expensive restaurant in the state of Georgia, was praised for its Southern hospitality, celebrated for its unique seasonal menu and envied for its esteemed clientele. But what Dionne loved most about the establishment was the romantic ambience. Vintage mirrors hung from the ivory walls, bronze candelabras showered the restaurant with light, and fine china beautified the round tables. The air held a savory scent, one that roused Dionne's hunger. Her mouth watered and her stomach grumbled at the tantalizing aromas wafting out of the kitchen.

Entering the waiting area, Dionne scanned the dining room. TV personalities, the mayor of Atlanta and socialites dripping in diamonds were living it up—eating, drinking and laughing as though there were no tomorrow. The patrons were illustrious, the mood was festive, and the silver-haired piano player was so talented, diners were moving and grooving in their seats.

"Welcome to Bacchanalia." The maître d', a slim man with blue eyes, gave a polite nod. "The private dining room is ready. Please follow me."

Dionne stepped forward, but Immanuel didn't move.

"A private room?" Wrinkles creased his forehead, and a scowl bruised his lips. "This is crazy. I should be treating *you* to dinner. Not the other way around."

Unsure of what to say in response, Dionne took a moment to gather her thoughts. In the limousine, on the drive over to Mastermind Operations, she'd rehearsed her speech to perfection, yet when she saw Immanuel her confidence deserted her. It was happening again. Her skin was cold and clammy, and her tongue was stuck to the roof of her mouth.

Hurry up, urged her inner voice. *Say something or he'll leave.*

Determined to salvage their date, Dionne moved closer to him and rested a hand on his arm. Damn. Like the rest of him appeared, it was hard, muscular and firm. Dionne blinked, chided herself to focus. It had taken several days to pull everything together, and she wasn't going to let anyone—not even the guest of honor—ruin her plans.

"You can pay for dinner next time." To lighten the mood, she added, "And I suggest you save up, because I have *very* expensive taste, and a *very* healthy appetite."

Immanuel didn't laugh. His mouth was set in a frown, and his arms were crossed.

"Dionne, I don't like this. This isn't me."

"You don't like what?"

"You paying for dinner. I'm old-school, and where I come from, men pay for everything."

"Well, I'm new school, and where I come from, women can do it all, *including* pay the check." Dionne inclined her body toward his, but didn't speak until he looked right at her. "You saved my life. If not for you, I wouldn't be here today. So please don't fight me on this—"

"You're giving me too much credit. I'm not a hero, Dionne. *You* are." Pride shone in his eyes. "You're my hero! You opened a can of whoop-ass on that creep, and I bet from now on he'll think twice about robbing innocent people."

"I sure hope so, because if he tries me again I won't go so easy on him."

"Let's meet halfway," he said, sliding his hands into the front pockets of his dress pants. "You pay for dinner, and I'll leave the tip. Deal?"

Dionne patted the lapel of his suit jacket. "Immanuel, don't worry. I got it."

"I insist."

"Are you always this difficult?"

"Yeah, I am," he confessed, wearing an impish smile. "I'm a Scorpio, *and* Italian, so you don't have a chance in hell of winning this argument."

"Fine, if it'll make you happy, you can leave the tip."

"I'm overjoyed."

"No," she challenged, pointing a finger at his chest. "You're a pain in the ass."

Chuckling, he took her hand in his and gave it a light squeeze. Desire prickled her skin. Dionne felt like the belle of the ball when Immanuel wrapped an arm around her waist and pulled her close to his side. He made her feel protected, as if her well-being mattered more than anything. It was a heady feeling.

Stealing a glance at him, Dionne admired his handsome profile. It was impossible to keep her eyes off him. He had a face made for magazines, a lean, toned physique, and a voice so sexy her ears tingled every time he spoke. He looked sexy in his slim-fitting navy suit, but it was how confidently he moved that captured the attention of every woman in the room. Immanuel Morretti was the hottest thing to come out of Italy since Versace, and he was with *her*. Dionne was proud to be his date, and not just because he was a hottie. He was a gentleman, a class act, the kind of guy women couldn't help but love.

Dionne spotted a familiar face across the dining room and strangled a groan. Adeline. *Someone* must *have it out for me*, she thought, drawing in a deep, calming breath. Jules's sister was a busybody who wasn't happy unless she was telling someone what to do. The executive accountant ran a tight ship at home, and everyone in the Fontaine family, including her toddler son, knew better than to cross her. Her eyes were daggers, and her lips were a hard line. As Adeline approached, Dionne stopped and nodded her head in greeting. "Hi, Adeline," she said with a polite smile. "How are you doing?"

"Scheming gold digger," she spat, through clenched teeth. Adeline brushed past her and continued through the restaurant with her friends—two successful business women Dionne had had in her home as guests on several occasions. The pair ignored her, but they made eyes at Immanuel.

"They looked happy to see you."

"The woman in the mauve cocktail dress is my ex's sister, and we don't get along."

"Why not?" he asked, raising an eyebrow.

"We're both opinionated, headstrong women. We clashed from day one."

Entering the private dining room, Dionne took in her surroundings. It was an elegant, intimate space filled with glass vases overflowing with long-stemmed red roses and scented candles. Stars twinkled, showering the space with a faint, sultry light. The crescent moon in the night sky provided a romantic backdrop.

Immanuel pulled out Dionne's chair. "Have a seat, beautiful."

"I love fine dining, and this meal is going to be epic, so the sooner we start eating the better."

Amusement twinkled in his eyes. "Epic, huh?"

"You just wait and see."

"A Hero's Dinner?" Frowning, he picked up the glossy white card on his plate and read the personalized menu aloud. "The Good Samaritan signature cocktail sounds interesting."

"You'll love it. It's made with Campari and orange juice and tastes a lot like Negroni."

"What do *you* know about Negroni? It's an Italian cocktail that's decades old."

"I know a little somethin' somethin' about Italian cuisine. I've done my research."

"Wow, I'm impressed. There's never a dull moment when you're around, is there?"

"I feel the same way about you, Mr. Morretti. A woman can never have too many male friends, and I love how honest and grounded you are."

He cocked a brow, examined her with a critical eye. "Why do you sound surprised?"

"Because it's hard to meet a man of integrity in this day and age."

"And women are perfect, right?"

"God no!" Dionne smirked. "Just me."

The waiter arrived, introduced himself and unloaded his wooden tray. "I will be back shortly with the second course," he said in a faint British accent. "Enjoy the appetizers."

Dionne picked up her cocktail glass and raised it in the air. "I'd like to make a toast."

"The floor is yours."

"Thank you for saving my life, and for being a kick-ass fairy godfather."

Immanuel cracked up. "No one's ever called me a fairy before."

"There's a first time for everything," she teased, shooting him a playful wink.

He laughed harder, and the sound of his hearty chuckle made Dionne smile. After the week she'd had, it felt good to joke around with Immanuel. "To friendship," she proposed, fervently nodding her head. "May we be friends for many years to come."

"I'll drink to that."

They shared a smile, then clinked glasses.

Dionne tasted her cocktail, deciding she liked the spicy flavor, then eagerly sampled the Kumamoto oysters. As they ate, they discussed their careers, their favorite cities and vacation spots, and their families. Immanuel listened more than he spoke, but as they started the second course he opened up to her about his past relationships. He was a sensitive man who felt things deeply, but he wasn't a crybaby by any means. He took responsibilities for the mistakes he'd made in the past, and was determined to be a better man. Dionne admired his drive and ambition.

"When was the last time you spoke to Emilio?" she asked, wondering what had caused the rift between the two brothers that Sharleen had once casually mentioned. "Have you seen him since you returned to Atlanta?"

"No, and I don't plan to. I have nothing to say to him."

"That's harsh."

His face hardened. "No, that's the truth."

"My sisters drive me crazy sometimes, but I couldn't imagine not having them in my life. Mel and Lorna are my best friends, and I love them dearly."

Immanuel nodded his head, as if he wholeheartedly

agreed. He chewed his food slowly, as if he was savoring every bite, then reached for his water glass.

"It's sad that you guys don't talk," she said, quietly. "Do you miss him?"

"Every day."

"Then why don't you call him?"

A dark shadow crossed his face. "Because what Emilio did is unforgivable."

"I don't believe that. Everyone deserves a second chance."

"Even family members who stab you in the back?"

"Yes, even family members who stab you in the back. Your family is a gift to you, as you are to them. You need each other, especially during tough times."

Immanuel fell silent. His head was down, his face was sad, and his posture was stiff.

It was hard for Dionne to keep her wits about her when all she wanted to do was take him in her arms and hold him tight. "It might help to talk about it."

"You wouldn't understand."

"I have a Masters in psychology. Try me."

"Emilio slept with my fiancée."

Dionne choked on her tongue and stared at him in astonishment. She hadn't expected him to drop a bombshell during dinner and was stunned by his confession. To alleviate the dryness in her throat, she picked up her glass and sipped her cocktail. Dionne couldn't think of anything to say in response, and needed a moment to get her thoughts in order.

"When I caught Emilio and Valentina in bed, I went ballistic."

"I'm not surprised you lost your cool. Anyone would in that situation."

"My brother and I fought like dogs that night." Immanuel touched his cheek, winced as if in pain. "This scar was a parting gift from him."

Moved by compassion, she offered a sympathetic smile. Immanuel wore a pensive expression on his face and seemed to be in another world. *Is Immanuel thinking about his ex-fiancée right now? Does he still love her? Does he wish he were having dinner with her tonight instead of me?*

Dionne banished the thoughts from her mind and returned to the present. She didn't like talking about Jules or the problems in their marriage, but maybe if she opened up to Immanuel he'd realize that he wasn't alone. Everyone faced tough times.

"I know how it feels to be betrayed by someone you love," she said quietly, meeting his gaze with her own. "For years, I suspected my husband was cheating on me, but I didn't have proof of his infidelity until his mistress showed up on my doorstep last year demanding money."

"You must have been devastated."

"Actually, I was relieved. Knowing the truth gave me the courage to move out and file for divorce." Dionne held her head high. "I've always believed disappointments are a blessing in disguise, and every setback I've faced has made me a stronger, more resilient person."

Immanuel gripped his glass in his hands, held it so hard his knuckles turned white.

"Have you ever asked Emilio why he betrayed you?"

"He said he didn't know Valentina was my girl," he said in a pained whisper.

"That sounds plausible. Why don't you believe him?"

"Because he's a spoiled, egotistical jerk who only cares about himself."

"People change, Immanuel."

"Not my brother. He's as selfish as they come."

Dionne hesitated, struggling with her words. She didn't want Immanuel to think she was taking sides, but it was important for her to speak her mind. "I've had dinner with Emilio and Sharleen on several occasions, and that wasn't my impression of him at all. He's chivalrous and charming, and his love and devotion for Sharleen are admirable."

Immanuel stared at her with astonishment, as if she were dancing on top of the table.

"What will it take for you to forgive Emilio?" she asked, wishing he'd stop glaring at her.

He answered with a shrug. "I don't know."

Silence fell across the table. It was deafening, thick with tension, and the longer it lasted the more uncomfortable Dionne felt.

"I'm mad at Emilio, but I'm even angrier at myself for choosing someone like Valentina. I thought she was 'the one,' and I feel like a jackass for proposing to her."

"Don't beat yourself up about it. That chapter of your life is over, and now it's time to learn and grow from that experience." Dionne parted her lips and was shocked by the pitiful sound of her voice. "Consider yourself lucky. At least you don't have two failed marriages under your belt. Now, *that's* hard to live down."

Immanuel paused reflectively, seemingly giving considerable thought to what she said. "What went wrong in your first marriage?"

"I was naive, and he was a worldly older man who swept me off my feet," she explained with a deep sigh. "Our differences drove us apart, and we eventually split up."

"How long were you married?"

"Two years. I was young and dumb and had no business tying the knot."

Dionne kept her eyes down, fiddled with the gold napkin holder beside her plate. She wondered what Immanuel would think if he knew the truth. *Would he think the worst of her? Would he keep his distance?* At the sound of his voice, she blinked.

"It sounds like you've overcome a lot of adversity in your life."

"Haven't we all?"

"That's certainly true in my case."

"Are you still in love your ex? Do you want to reconcile with her?" Holding her breath, she waited anxiously to hear his response. Not that it mattered. They were friends, and that would never change.

"It's been five years since our breakup."

"That's not what I asked you."

"No, I don't want her back, but I miss her companionship." His tone was somber. "It would be cool to have someone to spend time with at the end of a long workday."

"Then get a dog. They're fun and loyal and easy to please."

Immanuel chuckled. "You're hilarious."

And you're even sexier when you laugh.

His eyes probed hers, and his gaze made her skin flush with heat. Worried she had food on her face, Dionne grabbed her napkin and wiped her mouth. It didn't help. Immanuel continued to examine her with his bedroom eyes. "What is it?"

"Nothing." He reached across the table and touched her hand. "It's hard to believe we've only known each other for a week. I feel like I've known you for years."

Me, too. Even more shocking? I dream about you every single night.

The waiter appeared, carrying a white box tied with a red ribbon on his wooden tray, and presented the gift to Immanuel. "Sir, this is for you."

"I don't understand. What's going on?"

The waiter set the box down on the table in front of Immanuel and left.

Dionne felt warm and tingly all over, excited that her plan had gone off without a hitch.

"What is it?" he asked, pointing at the box.

"There's only one way to find out. Open it."

Immanuel picked up the box, untied the ribbon and placed the lid on the table. "A Rolex Submariner 16610V?" Surprise covered his face and seeped into his tone. "Where did you get this? It's a collector's piece worth thousands of dollars."

Dionne gave him a quizzical look. "Yeah, how do you know?"

"I bought one for my dad for Father's Day," he explained, wearing an impish smile. "My dad and I rarely speak, but I wasn't going to let Emilio upstage me again this year."

"Do you like it?"

"Yes, but I can't accept it. It's too expensive."

"You have to. Your name is inscribed on the back of it."

Frowning, he took the watch out of the box and turned it over. "To Immanuel, my hero." A smile curled the corners of his lips. "Thank you, Dionne. I'll wear it with pride."

Immanuel took her hand and tenderly kissed it, and her heart skipped and danced.

Three hours and seven courses later, Dionne and Immanuel left Bacchanalia. The impeccable service, creative food and exquisite wine pairings had exceeded her expectations. As they exited the private dining room Dionne thanked the staff for a wonderful evening. Everything was delicious, from the first bite to the last. It was, without a doubt, the best dining experience she'd ever had. And the best date, too. Charming and urbane, Immanuel regaled her with stories about his travels abroad, and after their third round of cocktails they were cracking jokes like longtime friends. Conversation flowed freely from one subject to the next, and no topic was off-limits. It was midnight, well past Dionne's bedtime, but she was wide-awake, ready to talk for hours more.

"Let's go to Polaris," Dionne suggested, exiting the restaurant on Immanuel's arm. The wind whistled through the trees, the air held a crisp, refreshing scent and the sky was painted a dazzling shade of pink. "They make delicious iced coffee drinks, and the rooftop view of the Atlanta skyline is breathtaking."

"Can I take a rain check? I have an early-morning meeting tomorrow, and if I want to impress the executives at Sony Music I need to get my rest."

"Sony Music?" she repeated, arching a brow. "Are you auditioning for a boy band?"

Immanuel pitched his head back and erupted in laughter.

"I didn't know you could sing. My, my, my, Mr. Morretti, you're full of surprises."

Resting a hand on her back, he opened the back door and helped her inside the limousine. "Sony Music wants to hire a new security firm," he explained, sitting down beside her. "They heard Mastermind Operations is the best in the business, and it is."

"I *love* your humility," she teased, unable to resist poking fun at him. "It's endearing."

"And I love your smile."

Thanks for giving me something to smile about. Immanuel was impossible not to like, and it was easy to see why his security firm was in high demand. He was everything a man should be—attentive, chivalrous and affectionate— and she enjoyed spending time with him.

The traffic was light, the streets were quiet, and as the limousine cruised down Peachtree Road, Dionne reflected on their romantic marathon date. She couldn't have asked for a better night, and wished their time together didn't have to end.

"Tonight was fun. We should do this again soon, but next time *I'm* paying for dinner."

"Don't even start. Your tip was three times the cost of our meal."

Immanuel grinned, shrugging his shoulders dismissively, and Dionne knew she'd been had. That bothered her. *Was he intimidated by her success? Is that why he'd left an exorbitant tip?*

Hearing his voice, she blinked and returned to the present.

"Do you have plans tomorrow?" Immanuel asked.

"Aren't you going to Demetri's game?"

His eyes narrowed in confusion. "*You're* going?"

"Yes, Sharleen invited me," she explained. "I don't follow baseball, but since your cousin is a baseball legend, I agreed to go."

"So, you're going to the game with Sharleen *and* Emilio?"

"Is that a problem?" she asked, confused by his odd reaction.

"No." He sighed and raked a hand through his hair. "I haven't seen my brother in years. It's bound to be an awkward reunion, and I'm not looking forward to it."

"Immanuel, if Emilio approaches you at the game, be open and honest about your feelings. Try to bury the hatchet once and for all."

Nodding his head as if he was considering her advice, he stroked the length of his jaw.

"I want you to come with me to the game."

"You do?" she blurted out.

"Yes, of course. You're great company, and I think we'll have fun together."

So do I. You make me feel like a teenager again.

"We can have dinner at one of the restaurants near Turner Field, then walk over to the stadium in time for the game. What do you say?"

Dionne wanted to cheer, but contained her excitement.

She was a mature, dignified woman, not a tween girl at a pop concert. "I'd love to."

"Great," he said smoothly, wearing a boyish grin. "It's a date."

I was hoping you'd say that, she thought, smiling. *Tomorrow can't come fast enough.*

The limo stopped in front of Dionne's house, and Immanuel helped her get out of the car. Taking her hand, he led her up the walkway. His touch, his smile and the scent of his cologne put her in the mood for loving. Dionne couldn't remember the last time she'd had sex. A year? Two? Jules used to complain she was cold and uptight in bed, but his insults never bothered her. He knew nothing about tenderness and intimacy, so who was he to judge? After learning about his affairs, she'd kicked him out of their bedroom and devoted all her time and energy to work. But tonight, Dionne didn't want to edit the monthly newsletter or read client profiles. She wanted one man in her bed, and his name was Immanuel Morretti.

Her heart was in turmoil; her body, too. She was hot and cold, nervous and excited, anxious and giddy, but the strongest emotion Dionne felt was desire. She longed to touch him, to caress him, wanted to taste his lips once and for all. Struggling to keep her hands at her sides and off his chest, she tore her gaze away from his mouth and took her keys out of her purse.

Dionne unlooked the door, flipped on the lights in the darkened foyer and disabled the alarm. She turned around to find Immanuel watching her and sucked in a deep breath.

His gaze was piercing, so intense and seductive that erotic images consumed her thoughts. She imagined them upstairs in her master bedroom, rolling around in bed, kissing each other desperately. But quickly changed the channel in her mind. They were buddies, not friends with benefits, and nothing good could ever come of having a fling with him. "I'm going to make myself a cup of coffee," she said, dropping her keys on the end table. "Would you like one?"

"No. I have to go, but I'll call you tomorrow." Immanuel leaned over, touched a hand to her face, and kissed her cheek. "Thanks for dinner. And, the watch."

Disappointed, Dionne watched him jog down the steps and duck inside the waiting limousine. She waved goodbye, and once the car drove off, she activated the alarm. With a heavy heart, she walked into the living room, collapsed onto the couch and stared up at the ceiling. She'd had a great time with Immanuel at Bacchanalia, and for as long as Dionne lived she'd never forget how special he made her feel. *And* how hot and bothered.

Chapter 9

"Let's not argue," Dionne said, raising her voice to be heard above the chatter in the conference room. It was Friday afternoon, and her staff—twelve life coaches, a receptionist and three bright-eyed interns—were seated around the table discussing mandatory employee training programs. They were snacking on fruit and the homemade pastries Sharleen had brought in, and drinking coffee as if there were no tomorrow. "We can revisit the issue in the future, but in the meantime everyone please register for the December training session."

Dionne glanced at Sharleen and laughed inwardly when her vice president tapped the face of her wristwatch and mouthed, "Move it along. We have plans tonight, remember?"

"Are there any questions?" Dionne asked, glancing around the table.

Annabelle raised her hand. "Are you okay?"

Confused by the question, she frowned and shot the

blonde a quizzical look. "Yes, of course, why wouldn't I be?"

"Because you were brutally attacked a week ago—"

Dionne cut her off. "What does that have to do with our monthly meeting?"

"Some staff members were wondering if your attack has something to do with your ongoing feud with your estranged husband," she explained, leaning forward in her chair. "A lot of people think Brad attacked you, but I don't believe that for a second. Brad isn't a criminal, and even though he was wrongly dismissed, I don't think he'd be stupid enough to attack you…"

Oh. No. She. Didn't! Dionne wanted to reach across the table and smack the novice life coach for embarrassing her, but she caught herself in time and buried her hands in her lap. Anger burned inside her. Her personal life was just that—personal—and she didn't appreciate Annabelle's asking about the attack during the staff meeting. It was unprofessional and disrespectful, but Dionne didn't lash out at her.

Dionne took a sip of her chamomile tea. Over the rim of her mug, she noticed that everyone in the room was staring at her intently, passing judgment with their eyes. Since she didn't want her employees to think she was upset, she put down her mug and spoke in a confident tone.

"Annabelle, I'm fine," she said, her voice masking her frustration. "I appreciate your concern, but the Atlanta Police Department is working hard on the case, and I'm confident they'll make an arrest soon."

Interest sparked in her eyes. "So, the police have a suspect?"

Dionne ignored her, consulting her two-page agenda instead. "Let's discuss our clients." Back in control, she straightened in her chair and picked up her pen. "I'd like everyone to give a brief update about the clients you're supporting, and the challenges you've faced this week."

Silence plagued the room, and staff members shifted around in their chairs.

"I'll start." Annabelle rose to her feet. Her expression was somber, but she spoke with pride. "I had a six o'clock session last night with Ryder Knoxx at his Druid Hills mansion, and he made another pass at me."

Dionne started to speak, then remembered the conversation she'd had with Immanuel at AT&T store last week and bit her tongue. His words played in her mind, and her anger abated. *You can catch more flies with honey than vinegar.*

"Thanks for sharing, Annabelle. It can be challenging working with celebrities, and I appreciate your efforts, and your candor," Dionne said, wearing a sympathetic smile. "Let's meet tomorrow to discuss the situation further. I'd love to share some tips and strategies with you that have served me well for the last fifteen years."

Annabelle beamed. "Thank you, Mrs. Fontaine. I'd like that very much."

Within seconds, everyone was talking, openly sharing their concerns and frustrations. For the next forty-five minutes, Dionne shared advice with her staff. Problem-solving was mentally draining, but she welcomed the challenge. This was her calling, what she was born to do, and she wanted to empower her staff more than anything.

"I want to thank you all for a job well done." Dionne made eye contact with each staff member, trying to communicate her gratitude and appreciation through her gaze. This was her favorite part of the day, what she loved most about her job. She liked touching base with her team, and looked forward to connecting with them every Friday at the monthly meeting. "Because of your efforts, Pathways Center is the number one life coaching center in Atlanta, and it's going to remain that way for many more years to come, right, everyone?"

Applause, cheers and whistles filled the room.

"Staff, that will be all for today." Closing her notebook, Sharleen gestured to the papers on the middle of the table. "Please remember to submit your holiday requests to the HR department by Friday if you'd like time off during Thanksgiving. It's only a few weeks away, so time is of the essence."

Everyone filed out of the room, and Sharleen locked the door.

"Who are you and what have you done with my boss?"

Dionne laughed out loud. "What's gotten into you?"

"I was about to ask *you* the same question. I thought you were going to strangle Annabelle when she asked you about the attack, but you handled it like a pro. And you were surprisingly sympathetic when she shared her concerns about Ryder Knoxx."

"I've turned over a new leaf—"

"I'd say," she snapped, nodding her head emphatically. "The old Dionne would have given her a thorough tongue-lashing, then tossed her out the door!"

Laughing, Dionne leaned back in her chair and crossed her legs. Since the attack, she'd changed for the better. She was more patient, less uptight, and Immanuel was the reason why. He never raised his voice, treated everyone with respect and went out of his way to help others. He was a kind, gentle soul, the type of person she aspired to be. She was glad they had met. Not only was he a great friend, he was someone she could count on.

"I know I can be hard on people, especially our female staff, so I'm making a concerted effort to be more understanding," she confessed, speaking from the heart. "To make Pathways Center a success I need the support of the entire team, and since you can catch more flies with honey than vinegar, I'm killing them with kindness."

"I've been saying that for years," Sharleen said, fervently nodding her head. "I'm glad you're finally taking my advice. It's about time."

Hearing her cell phone vibrate, Dionne picked it up off the table and read her newest text message. It was from Immanuel, and as she read his message, heat flooded her body.

I can't wait to see you. You've been on my mind all day.

Her heart fluttered inside her chest. Immanuel made her feel special, as if his sole purpose in life were to please her. Since their candlelit dinner at Bacchanalia he'd been doing just that. On Sunday, he took her to see *Motown: The Musical* at the Atlanta Theater, then days later they had lunch at her favorite sushi spot, and last night he'd treated her to dessert at Sugar Shack, a quaint Brookhaven shop just minutes away from her house. They'd sat at their corner table talking about movies, music and past relationships for hours. By the time they left the café, she was dying to kiss him. At her doorstep, he'd given her a hug and a peck on the cheek, but she'd secretly longed for more. She wanted to kiss him, and yearned to feel his hands all over her body. Friendship be damned. Everything about Immanuel was a turn-on—his piercing eyes, his panty-wetting smile, the way he moved—and it was getting harder and harder for Dionne to fight the desires of her flesh.

"Why are you smiling from ear to ear?" Sharleen asked, wearing an amused expression on her face. "Did you finally sign a celebrity for our new marketing campaign?"

"No, not yet, but I'm working on it."

"Do you want me to ask Emilio to do the ad?"

Dionne couldn't resist poking fun at her friend and hid

a cheeky smile. "No, don't, it's *never* a good idea to mix business with pleasure."

"Says who? Mixing business with pleasure worked for me, and I have the engagement ring to prove it!" Sharleen laughed. "We better get going. Emilio should be here any minute to pick us up for Demetri's game, and I don't want to make my baby wait."

"You guys go on without me. I'll just meet you at Turner Field."

"But we agreed to go together, and you won't be granted access to Demetri's luxury box without us," she explained.

"I know, but Immanuel invited me to the game and I said yes."

"Immanuel!" She dropped into her chair, wheeled over to where Dionne was sitting at the head of the table and gripped her shoulders. Her face was bright, her eyes were wild with excitement, and her voice was a deafening shriek. "You guys are dating? No way! OMG, if you guys get married we'll be sisters-in-law! How cool is that!"

"Girl, slow your roll. It's not like that. We're just friends."

"Yeah, for now, but it's just a matter of time before Immanuel sweeps you off your feet."

Sadness pierced her heart, and a bitter taste filled her mouth. "I hope not, because the last time I fell in love I was played for a fool."

"This time will be different."

"How do you know?"

"Because I know you," she insisted, her tone firm and convincing. "You're smarter and wiser now, and besides, Immanuel's a Morretti, and Morretti men don't mistreat women."

Dionne smirked. "What, so you're the family spokesperson now?"

"Nope. I'm just a hopeless romantic who's a sucker for happy endings."

"Then forget about my love life, and focus on reuniting Emilio with his brother."

Her smile dimmed. "There's nothing I can do. Trust me, I've tried."

"Has Emilio tried reaching out to Immanuel?"

"Only a million times. He calls and texts him, but to no avail. Immanuel has completely shut him out of his life. No matter what Emilio does, it's never good enough."

"I know the feeling." Dionne released a deep sigh. "You heard my sisters. They think I'm to blame for Jules's infidelity and ordered me to call off the divorce and return home."

"I'm glad I don't have older siblings, because I hate when people tell me what to do," Sharleen said. "What do your parents think? Do they want you to reconcile with Jules?"

"Yes, unfortunately they do. I went home on Saturday, and my dad had some very harsh words for me. He stopped short of calling me irresponsible, but his comments still hurt."

"I'm sorry to hear that, but try not to let it get you down." Sharleen winked and gave her a one-armed hug. "I think you're fabulous, and I bet Immanuel does, too."

Laughing, the women exited the conference room. They parted ways in the reception area, and after Dionne spoke to the receptionist she grabbed the day's mail and marched out the front door. It was early evening, but the sun was shining and the air was warm.

Her cell phone rang and she put it to her ear, thinking it was Immanuel. "Hello?"

Click.

Annoyed, she stared down at the phone in disgust. The prank calls had started the day after she'd arrived home from the hospital, and had increased in frequency ever since. Her cell phone provider said there was nothing it could do and advised her to change her number. Dionne considered telling Immanuel about the calls, but struck the thought from her mind. They were both busy, with a million things to do, and she didn't want her problems to add to his stress.

Dionne glanced at her watch. She had just enough time to go home and freshen up before Immanuel picked her up for their date. An image of him clad in an Armani suit flashed in her mind, and a shiver tickled her spine. They were friends and nothing more, so why did the thought of seeing him again excite her?

Because he's kind and chivalrous and you have a lot in common, whispered her inner voice. *Immanuel treats you like a person, not an object, and it's refreshing to be with someone who appreciates your mind, not just your body.*

Dionne picked up her pace. Anxious to see Immanuel, she rushed over to her rental car, hopped inside and sped out of the parking lot.

Chapter 10

The private luxury suite at Turner Field was filled with gorgeous furniture, flat-screen TVs and a chic marble bar. Sports memorabilia lined the sable-brown walls, and glass windows provided an unobstructed view of the field. Pop music played from the mounted speakers, and when Dionne heard the opening bar of her favorite Prince song a smile overwhelmed her mouth. Years ago, when she was in graduate school, her sisters had surprised her with tickets to his Atlanta show. They'd danced all night, sang off-key to each hit and screamed like teenage girls. Dionne thought about Mel and Lorna and wondered how they were doing. She hadn't spoken to them since they'd visited her home and left in a huff, but she planned to call them tomorrow. Surely they weren't still mad at her—

"Is everything okay? You suddenly went quiet on me…"

Hearing Immanuel's voice, Dionne blinked and met his gaze.

That was her first mistake.

Touching his arm was her second.

Inhaling his cologne, her third.

Time screeched to a halt, and everything in the room faded to the background. He rested a hand on top of hers, splayed his fingers against her flesh, and her body trembled with desire. Immanuel looked at her as if she was hot, desirable, the sexiest woman he'd ever seen. His grin, the one that sparked in his eyes and warmed his lips, made her clit tingle and her panties wet.

His touch made her dizzy and her thoughts scatter, but she didn't pull away. She didn't have the willpower it required, not after all the flirting and touching they'd been doing since he picked her up at home. Dionne was drawn to Immanuel, loved being with him, and could easily spend the rest of the night playing this thrilling game of cat-and-mouse. When it came to the opposite sex, she'd always had a will of steel, more self-control than a man of the cloth, but Immanuel excited her, turned her on like no one else, and flirting with him was the ultimate rush. *Is it just a matter of time before we become lovers?* she wondered, her heart racing at the thought. *Is this the night he'll finally make his move?*

Dionne licked her lips. Her gaze left his face and slid down his ripped physique. His shoulders filled out each inch of his white mock-neck shirt. His dark straight-leg jeans were a perfect fit, and his Timberland boots gave him a bad-boy edge, one that made her nipples harden and her body quiver. Embarrassed by her physical reaction to him, she turned away and reached for her cocktail glass. "I'm good," she said, tasting her martini. "Some game, huh?"

"What game? I'm having so much fun with you I forgot who was playing."

His eyes zeroed in on her face, held her in their powerful grip. The energy pulsing between them was insane, more potent than a shot of vodka and impossible to resist.

Immanuel was the sexiest man ever, and there was an air of mystery about him that she was inexplicably drawn to.

"You look incredible tonight," he whispered. "Every night, actually."

Immanuel put a hand on her leg, and her pulse shifted into overdrive.

"Are you having a good time?"

"Of course," she said, returning his smile. "I always have a good time with you."

"Great answer."

They had sat on stools in front of the window when they arrived hours earlier, and even though Dionne didn't know anything about baseball, she was having a great time. The mood was festive, charged with excitement, and laughter abounded. "Is your cousin's fiancée here?" she asked, noting all of the attractive women in the room. "Sharleen thinks Angela's the best thing since fat-free ice cream, and I'd love to meet her. She sounds like good people."

"No, Angela's not here. She's a sports nut who likes to be close to all the action, so she watches from the stands with Demetri's overzealous fans."

Dionne heard a brash, horselike laugh, recognized it immediately and rolled her eyes. She could spot a dog a mile away, and Immanuel's business partner needed to be in a kennel. Malcolm was strutting around the room with his chest puffed out, bopping from one woman to the next, acting like he owned the place.

"This game sucks. And so does the home team," Malcolm bellowed, taking a swig of his beer. "Demetri's killing the Astros tonight. There's no way in hell they can make a comeback."

Malcolm plopped down on the stool beside Immanuel, and Dionne swallowed a groan. It surprised her the men were not only business partners, but longtime friends. They couldn't be more different. Immanuel was suave, cultured and refined, the kind of man people gravitated toward. Malcolm was loud and juvenile, the type of man women ran away *from*, not to.

"Are you ready to bounce?" Malcolm asked. "Let's go check out the 69 Club."

Immanuel's narrowed gaze and wrinkled nose spoke of his displeasure. "We're too old for that bar. Most of the clientele are underage, and—"

"Like hell I am. I don't look a day over twenty-five."

Laughter exploded from Dionne's mouth. Both men turned to look at her, their eyebrows raised. She didn't like Malcolm, but since she didn't want to make any enemies, she simmered down.

"Dionne, you enjoy having a good time, right?" Smiling with the likeness of a snake, he ogled her chest. "Want to check out a hot new club?"

His question was ridiculous. As if. *Why would she want to go to a sleazy nightclub on the wrong side of town when she'd rather be alone with Immanuel?* They'd had great conversations about life and love, and the more Dionne learned about him the more she wished he were her man. "Thanks for the invitation, but I'll pass. I'm not the club type."

Rap music began to play, and Malcolm hopped to his feet. "I'll be back in a few." He put his cell phone to his ear and swaggered off.

Dionne spotted Sharleen and Emilio standing at the bar, and waved in greeting. They made an attractive couple in their Chicago Royals attire, and were gazing at each other with stars in their eyes. "Sharleen and Emilio are here. Let's go say hi."

"I'm good here. You go ahead."

"Come on," she said, dragging him up to his feet. "Don't be like that."

"Don't be like what?"

"An old sourpuss!"

His nose twitched, but he didn't laugh.

"Fine, I'll text Sharleen and ask them to come to us."

"If Emilio knows what's good for him, he'll stay on his side of the room."

"Immanuel, no one likes a bully."

"Who are you calling a bully?"

"You," Dionne said, pointing a finger at his chest. "And it's not cool."

"I'm not a bully."

"Then prove me wrong." Dionne tilted her head to the side and wore a knowing smile. "Be the kind, chivalrous gentleman your grandmother raised you to be, and every woman in here will be eating out of your hands."

"I don't want to impress anyone but you."

"Then let's have a drink with your brother and his gorgeous fiancée."

Dionne grabbed her purse, tucked it under her arm and walked purposely toward the bar. In her peripheral version, she saw Immanuel behind her and cheered inwardly. "I thought you'd never get here," she said, approaching Sharleen. "What took you guys so long? I was worried you'd changed your mind about coming tonight."

"I wanted to be here sooner, but my boss left work early again today, and I had to lock up." Wearing a long face, she sighed dramatically. "Girl, pray for me. She's *such* a tyrant."

"Emilio, are you sure Sharleen's the one?" Dionne asked. "She's a *real* handful."

"I'm a hundred percent sure. She's my everything, and I won't live without her."

The couple melted into each other's arms and shared a kiss.

Dionne waited for Emilio and Immanuel to acknowledge each other's presence, but they didn't. Thankfully, Sharleen did.

"Immanuel! It's great to finally meet you!" Speaking in Italian, she leaned in and kissed him on each cheek. "I thought this day would never come! I've heard a lot about you—"

"None of it's true."

Stunned, Dionne cranked her head to the right and examined Immanuel's profile. His voice was filled with animosity, and his face was dark with rage. His hands were curled into fists, and his mouth was a hard line. *What can I do to help?* she thought, her gaze darting between the two men. Dionne feared if she didn't do something quick, the situation was going to go from bad to worse. She quickly linked arms with Sharleen and moved away from the bar. "We're going to the ladies' room. We'll be back in a few."

Sharleen frowned. "We are? But I just got here, and the calamari smells *so* good."

"Don't worry," she whispered. "I'll buy you some at the concession stand. Let's go."

Immanuel wanted to beg her to stay, but he couldn't get his lips to work. Damn, Dionne had set him up and he hadn't even see it coming. His eyes tracked her through the room, sliding down her delicious curves and hips. Her short Chicago Royals baseball jersey showed off her toned arms, her skinny jeans made her ass look fantastic, and her high heels elongated her legs. His mind started to scheme and plot on how to get the exotic beauty into his bed permanently.

Dionne is still legally married, reminded his inner voice. *That means she's off-limits.*

Standing at the bar with his brother—the man who'd betrayed his trust and crushed his dreams—he felt his temperature rise and his pulse pound violently in his ears. But this wasn't the time or the place to have it out with Emilio, so he turned away.

Emilio caught his arm, gripped it tight.

His body stiffened. His first impulse was to push him away, but he remembered the advice Dionne had given him at Bacchanalia and took a deep, calming breath. Immanuel hated to admit it, but she was right. His feud with Emilio had gone on long enough. It was a struggle, but he kept his anger in check. "Get your hands off me."

"Immanuel, we need to talk."

"I have nothing to say to you."

"Fine. I'll talk. You listen."

He wheeled around and was surprised to see sadness flicker across Emilio's face. He looked troubled, as if he carried the weight of the world on his shoulders. *Was Emilio genuinely sorry about what he'd done? Had he learned his lesson?* Immanuel rejected his thoughts. He knew better. His brother was just putting on a show for his pretty fiancée. Emilio had hit the jackpot, which was no surprise. His brother was accustomed to dating—and stealing—beautiful women, and Sharleen was a stunner.

"Make it quick. I want to get back to the game."

"I never meant to hurt you."

"You slept with my fiancée. What did you *think* would happen?"

"I had no idea Valentina was your girl."

Immanuel scoffed and folded his arms across his chest. "Likely story."

"It's true. I didn't see you arrive at the party together that night. I was hyped about winning another championship, and when she stepped up to me in the game room, I…"

Emilio broke off speaking, but Immanuel filled in the blanks.

"You couldn't resist her charm, is that it?"

"Immanuel, I've changed. I'm not the man I used to be."

"I'm happy to hear that, because you used to be a jerk."

"Thanks, bro. I can always count on you to keep it real," Emilio said with a wry smile.

On the flat-screen television mounted above the bar, Immanuel watched players and coaches on each team shaking hands, and knew the game was over. Demetri and his team had pulled off another impressive win, and he was proud of his cousin. Immanuel glanced around the suite in search of Dionne, but couldn't find her anywhere. *Were guys chasing her down at every turn? Had she met someone at the concession stand? Were they exchanging numbers and—*

"The things you said at the funeral…" Emilio hung his head. "They almost killed me."

"I was way out of line. I'm sorry." Immanuel looked away. Had to. Talking about Lucca, his beloved nephew, made his heart ache. Since he didn't want to have an emotional breakdown at Turner Field he changed the subject. "Congratulations on your win at the World Series All-Star Race. It was a tough course, but you made it look easy."

Surprise colored his cheeks. "You were watching?"

"Of course. You're my brother. I always want you to crush the competition." He added. "I just don't want you to screw my girl."

"Damn, bro, that was harsh."

His eyes strayed to the door, and every time it opened he felt a rush of adrenaline. He missed Dionne and wanted her back at his side. They'd known each other only a couple weeks, but she was important to him. She appealed to him in every way, and he loved to be with her.

"I heard what you did for Dionne. Good looking out, bro."

"I didn't do anything. *She* beat the mugger until he was black and blue, not me."

"You know she's married to Jules Fontaine, right? The CFO of Fontaine Enterprises."

Immanuel nodded. "I know, but they're getting a divorce."

"It doesn't take a year to get a divorce."

"What are you saying?"

"Nothing, bro. Just be careful. I don't want you to get hurt again."

Then stay away from Dionne, he thought sourly. "I'm a big boy. I can handle myself."

"We're back." Sharleen snuggled against Emilio and wrapped her arms around his waist. "Baby, I missed you."

"Not as much as I missed you. It felt like you were gone for hours."

Immanuel wanted to gag, but he wore a blank expression on his face instead. He had to find Dionne. A floral scent tickled his nostrils, and he knew she was nearby. The thought heartened him, and when he spotted her behind him, he smiled in satisfaction.

"Did you guys talk?" Dionne asked. "Is everything okay?"

"We're cool." Immanuel took her hand. "The game just ended. Are you ready to go?"

"We're meeting up with Demetri and Angela for drinks," Emilio said.

Sharleen piped up. "We're going glow bowling in Buckhead. You two should come."

"We'd love to."

"We would?" Immanuel pulled Dionne aside and spoke in a quiet voice. He wanted to see his cousin and meet his bride-to-be, but he wasn't hanging out with Emilio. It was too much, too soon. "We can't go to Buckhead. We have plans with Malcolm."

"That's fine. No worries," Dionne said, letting go of his hand. "You go hang out with Malcolm, and I'll ask Emilio and Sharleen to drop me off after bowling."

Dionne stepped past him as if the matter were decided, but Immanuel caught her around the waist. "Not so fast." He stared down at her, wishing he could taste her luscious red lips. "We came together, we leave together. Understood?"

"Absolutely," she said with a sly wink, playfully jabbing a finger in his chest. "Now, let's bowl. You better bring your A game, or you're dead meat!"

Chapter 11

"I thought I was big and bad until I went toe-to-toe with this sexy pit bull in a skirt," Demetri joked. "Angela gave me a thorough tongue-lashing that day, and two years later my brothers and teammates still tease me about our studio showdown."

Dionne laughed out loud. The baseball star and his fiancée, Angela Kelly, were a hilarious twosome. Listening to Demetri recount the first time they met was the funniest thing she'd ever heard. Immanuel was sitting beside her on the leather couch, and the sound of his hearty chuckles warmed her heart. He held her close to his side, making her feel cherished and adored. *I could so get used to this,* she thought, leaning comfortably against him. *It feels like heaven being in his arms.*

The group was at the Painted Pin, an upscale entertainment bar in Buckhead's Miami Circle. The bar had it all. Valet parking, interactive games, and comfortable seating areas with candlelit tables and attractive furniture. It was a favorite neighborhood hangout, and the patrons—a mix of tourists, college students and couples—were enjoying everything the venue had to offer. Demetri's bodyguard, an ex-marine with a boxer's build, stood at the entrance of the VIP lounge keeping the groupies at bay. Fans of Emilio and Demetri were screaming their names and snapping pictures, but the cousins seemed unfazed by the attention.

"I thought Angela was going to whup my ass when I confronted her at WJN-TV," Demetri confessed. "And that would have been a disaster, because this face is worth millions!"

Everyone at the table laughed.

"That *can't* be a true story. It sounds like an episode of a reality TV show," Dionne said, dabbing at her eyes with her fingertips. "I think you guys are pulling my leg."

"You do, huh?" Demetri winked at Angela. "Baby, show her the footage."

"Footage!" Dionne and Sharleen shouted in unison. "What footage?"

Angela took her cell phone out of her purse, tapped the screen several times, then raised it in the air. "Since you asked," she said, with a knowing smile, "here it is."

Leaning forward in her seat, Dionne stared in horror—and amusement—as an online video titled "Sexy Chicago Newscaster Goes Off on Baseball Superstar" played on the screen.

"Damn, coz, Angela gave it to you good." Immanuel shook his head as if he couldn't believe it. "Next time your manager tells you not to do something, you should listen to him!"

Demetri stared down at Angela, his eyes shimmering with love and adoration. "I'm glad I disregarded Lloyd's advice, because meeting Angela was the best thing to ever happen to me. If I had to do it all over again, I would."

Demetri hugged Angela to his side and kissed her lips.

Dionne had never met a cuter couple, though Emilio and Sharleen were definitely giving Demetri and Angela a run for their money. They couldn't keep their hands off each other, and if Sharleen moved any closer to Emilio she'd be sitting in his lap. The couples were so smitten with each other. Dionne could actually feel the love in the air.

"You guys have been engaged forever," Emilio teased. "When's the big day?"

Angela beamed. "We're getting married next summer."

"And this time I'm not letting you postpone it." Demetri's tone was firm, and his eyes were narrowed in determination. "We're getting hitched next year come hell or high water."

"Hey!" Angela shrieked, pulling out of his arms. "What's *that* supposed to mean?"

"Baby, I'm just keeping it real. I was ready to marry you last year, but you just *had* to go to the White House and interview the president and first lady for your Christmas special."

Scowling, she poked a finger in his chest. "But you told me to do it."

"Of course I did," he said with a wink. "That's what a caring, supportive fiancé does for the woman he loves, but if you postpone the wedding again I'm withholding the lovin'!"

Dionne burst out laughing for the second time within minutes, and water filled her eyes. *The Morretti men are the real deal*, she thought, glancing around the table. Demetri and Emilio were sensitive, romantic men who loved to spoil their women, and it amazed her how open and honest they were about their feelings.

"How is Rafael?" Immanuel asked. "Every time I call his cell goes straight to voice mail."

"That's because he's knee-deep in dirty diapers!"

Demetri chuckled. "He's got his hands full with Violet, and he recently found out they're expecting baby number two."

Sharleen raised a brow. "Another baby? Wow. Their daughter is only eight months old."

"They're making up for lost time," Angela explained with a laugh. "Paris wants a big family, and I have a feeling they'll be a family of eight in no time."

"What about you guys?" Emilio asked. "Do you have any plans to increase the fold?"

"No, not yet, but we're getting plenty of practice."

Angela touched Demetri's face and pecked him on the lips. "*That* we are."

The waiter arrived, dropped off another round of drinks and appetizers, and sped off.

"Are we going to bowl or what?" Emilio rubbed his hands together. "I have an ass-whuppin' with your name on it, Demetri, and this time I won't go easy on you. The winner gets bragging rights *and* cash, so put your money where your mouth is."

Immanuel barked a laugh. "I'm in! You're *both* due for a beat down, so let's do this."

Dionne watched as the men got up from the couch and stalked over to lane seven, leaving the women behind. "Dionne, how come you're not eating?" Angela asked. "You don't like junk food?"

"Girl, please. Look at me. Do I *look* like the health-conscious type to you?"

The women laughed and clinked cocktail glasses. Dionne had few female friends, and had always turned to her sisters for advice and support. But right now, she enjoyed having girl talk with Sharleen and Angela. The Chicago newscaster was full of life and positive energy, and one of the most down-to-earth people Dionne had ever met. Add to that, she looked like a superstar. Silky black hair kissed her shoulders, her makeup was flawless, and her backless purple dress was fresh off the runway.

"Immanuel took me out for dinner before the game, and I ate enough for two," she said with a laugh. "If I keep pigging out I won't be able to fit into my dress for the wedding, and I paid big bucks for my Alexander McQueen gown."

"Girl, I hear you. I've gained twenty pounds since meeting Demetri, and it's all his fault. He's constantly feeding me, and I have no self-control when it comes to Italian cuisine. I love it all, especially the desserts, and my man's the most amazing cook ever!"

"Be thankful your wedding isn't six weeks away. I still have ten pounds to lose, but the more I diet the more I gain weight. It's like the universe is conspiring against me!" Sharleen said, excitement lacing her tone.

"Don't worry," Angela said reassuringly, rubbing her friend's shoulders. "You're going to be a beautiful bride, and Emilio won't be able to keep his eyes off you."

I know the feeling, Dionne thought, glancing at lane seven in search of Immanuel. She found him standing beside the scorer's table watching her and waved in greeting. He flashed a boyish smile, one that made his baby blues twinkle, and her heart leaped for joy. His gaze captured hers in a seductive grip, and all she could do was stare. Dionne rested a hand on her chest to calm her raging heartbeat, but it didn't help. Her pulse continued to race and pound.

"I love the story of how you and Immanuel met," Angela gushed. "It's *so* romantic."

"We're just friends."

"Sure you are, girl. Just keep telling yourself that."

"Angela, she's in denial," Sharleen said. "It happened to me, too."

"And me," Angela confessed, raising a hand in the air.

"Dionne, quit resisting Immanuel and join the 'He Swept Me Off My Feet' club, because once a Morretti man sets his sights on you, it's game over!"

The thought should have scared her, especially in light of her failed marriages, but it didn't. Dionne trusted her instincts and made it a point to listen to her gut feeling. Her heart was telling her Immanuel was someone special. The past two weeks had proved as much. He was unlike anyone she'd ever met, a brave, courageous man any woman would love to have.

Including you, whispered her inner voice.

Dionne heard her cell phone buzz, saw that she had a new text message from Mel and frowned. What the hell? Her sister's message was confusing, didn't make any sense.

Are you nearby? Text me when you get here.

Convinced the message was intended for someone else, she typed a message in response. Seconds later, her cell phone rang. "Hey, Mel. What's up?"

"Where are you?"

"Out with friends." Her gaze fell across Immanuel, and she smiled.

"The Fontaine Family Charity drive is tonight at Friendship House. You should be here."

Dionne was annoyed that her sister was yelling at her, but she kept her temper in check. She was having a great time with Immanuel and his family, and she wasn't going to let anyone ruin her night. "Mel, I have to go."

"So you're on your way?" Her sister sighed in relief, speaking in her usual bright and cheery tone. "Thank God. How long will it take you to get here?"

"Jules and I are getting a divorce, Mel. Our lives aren't intertwined anymore."

"You have to come. The entire family is here, and besides, it's for a good cause," she argued. "Adeline has worked tirelessly for Friendship House for decades, and she needs our support to make the charity drive a success."

Dionne nodded her head in agreement, but she didn't vocalize her thoughts. Her sister-in-law's work with inner-city youth was commendable, but the socialite was as spiteful as they come. Dionne didn't want anything to do with her. Over the years, Adeline had humiliated her countless times, and she shuddered at the memory of the tongue-lashing she'd given her last year for wearing a sleeveless dress to an event at the Fontaine family church. "Mel, I'll call you later."

She heard whispering, a shuffling sound, then Lorna's voice on the line.

"Are you with your new lover?" she demanded, her anger evident. "I spoke to Adeline, and she's very upset. She said you're flaunting him all over town. Dionne, how could you!"

Dionne stared down at the phone, stunned by her sister's words. Who did Lorna think she was? How dare she scream at her! Not wanting her friends to overhear her conversation, she excused herself from the table and left the lounge. She strode past the entrance and out the front door.

"You're jeopardizing your marriage," she continued. "Don't you see that? If Jules finds out you're hooking up with other men he'll never take you back—"

"Good, because our marriage is over, and I want a divorce."

"You don't mean that."

"Yes. I. Do." Dionne started to explain, to tell Lorna how she felt about Immanuel, but she stopped herself before the words left her mouth. She loved her sister and valued her opinion, but she didn't owe her an explanation. It was her life, her decision, and there was no way in hell she was going to the charity drive. "I have to get back to my friends. They're waiting for me."

"You're choosing some guy you just met over your family?"

"No, for once I'm doing what makes me happy, instead of doing what *you* want me to—"

Dionne didn't realize she was shouting or crying until she felt a hand on her back and heard Immanuel's voice behind her. He whispered in her ear, told her everything was going to be okay, tenderly stroking her shoulders.

"Lorna, I have to go. Bye."

Hanging up the phone, she cleaned her cheeks with the back of her hand. Dionne swallowed hard, but the lump in her throat seemed to grow, not shrink.

The wind whistled through the trees, blowing leaves in the sky, and the crisp, refreshing scent of autumn perfumed the night air. Chilled to the bone, Dionne hugged her arms to her chest.

"What are you doing out here?" Embarrassed that he'd caught her crying, she couldn't look at him, fearing she'd crumble if she did. She could feel him staring at her and attempted to dodge his gaze. "You're supposed to be inside."

"I got worried when I saw you leave and wanted to ensure you were okay."

"A hero's job is never done, is that it?"

Immanuel slid his hands around her shoulders. She felt warm and cozy in his arms, as if she were wrapped in a thick blanket. Her senses spun out of control; she was overwhelmed by his closeness, by his intimate caress. The air was electrified, perfumed with the scent of her desire. Her feelings were in tumult, her emotions, too—had been since the day she woke up in the hospital and saw Immanuel for the first time.

"Dionne, what's wrong? Who upset you?"

It was his tone, the gentle urging of his voice, that did

her in, that incited lustful thoughts. But she gathered herself and regained control. "It's not important."

"Yes it is, because you're important to me."

Dionne reluctantly pulled out of his arms. If she didn't put some distance between them she'd end up crossing the line, and the last thing she wanted to do was embarrass herself. To lighten the mood, she said, "I'm an amazing bowler. Want to see my moves?"

"Absolutely." Immanuel raised her hand to his mouth and kissed it. "Bring it on!"

Chapter 12

"If that's your take on love and relationships, you'll never meet Mrs. Right, because twenty-first century women can take care of themselves." Cradling the cordless phone between her ear and shoulder, Dionne entered the kitchen and lowered the temperature on the stove. The air smelled of spices and Italian herbs. The aroma was so enticing that she couldn't wait to eat.

Noticing the time on the stove, her eyes widened. After work, she'd gone to her evening spin class but she had so much on her mind she hadn't been able to focus. At home, her problems continued. Instead of doing housework, or packing for her upcoming business trip to Seattle, she'd flopped onto the couch, and called Immanuel. They talked two, sometimes three times a day. Their conversations lasted for hours. Chatting with him about her day always made Dionne feel better.

"All I'm saying is I liked it better when the roles were clearly defined," Immanuel said, fervently arguing his case.

"If we go out on a date I don't want you to drive, or order for us, or pay the bill, either. That's my job, not yours."

"Job? I think you're taking this whole chivalry thing too far."

"I think you're jaded and a bit cynical about men."

Hell yeah I am! You'd be jaded too if you'd been screwed over numerous times by the opposite sex. The only men who haven't played me are my father and brother.

"I love that you're a self-made woman, but I don't want you to spend money when you're with me. I got you, okay?"

Dionne winced, swallowing hard to alleviate the lump in her throat. She hated the expression *self-made woman*, and knew the term didn't apply to her. What would Immanuel think if he knew the truth? Would he think less of her? As he spoke, a frown crimped her lips. "So if I invited you to Bacchanalia again you'd say no?"

"Of course not. Smart, captivating women are my weakness, *and* you're a stunner."

"Good answer! I thought I was going to have to cut you!" she said with a laugh. One minute they were talking about their favorite pasta recipes, and the next thing Dionne knew they were having an intense discussion about love and relationships. Immanuel was an old-school gentleman who still believed females were the weaker sex, and Dionne enjoyed schooling him about career women. Talking with Immanuel took her mind off her troubles—her argument with her sisters, her stress at work, and her upcoming meeting at Simmons & Sons Law Firm. She laughed so hard at his jokes, her jaw ached. "If I ask you out—"

Immanuel cut her off. "I'll go, but I'm driving, *and* I'm paying the tab."

"That's silly. It doesn't matter who drives or who picks up the check."

"It does to me. My grandmother raised me to be a gentleman, and I take great pride in taking care of the women in my life. That's the Morretti way…"

His words impressed her, and the more he spoke about his role as a man and his duty to care for and protect women, the more Dionne wished she were his girlfriend. It wasn't the first time she'd had that thought, and probably wouldn't be the last. Loyal, sensitive men had always been her weakness, and Immanuel was everything she'd ever wanted in a man. He was opinionated and outspoken, and she loved debating with him about hot-button issues.

As Dionne made dinner, they conversed about work, getting tickets for the improv show at Comedy Club Atlanta, and meeting up with Sharleen and Emilio tomorrow night. It had been three weeks since their group date to the bowling alley, and although there was still tension between the two brothers, Immanuel was more open about seeing Emilio. He had no choice. Dionne made a point of "running into" the couple whenever they were out, and would convince Immanuel to join them for a drink. She was looking forward to having Thanksgiving dinner at Emilio's Greensboro estate.

A sharp pain stabbed her heart. This year, Lorna was hosting family dinner, but Dionne didn't feel comfortable going to her sister's home. Not after the heated argument they'd had at her parents' house last Sunday night. Since Immanuel wasn't welcome at Lorna's home, she'd decided to spend the holiday with her friends. Her parents didn't like it, thought she was being unreasonable, but there was nothing they could say to change her mind.

"How is the new car?"

"You don't even have to ask," she said, a smile overwhelming her lips. "I love it."

Last weekend, he'd picked her up at noon, and after dim sum in Chinatown they'd gone to a local car dealership. She'd fallen in love with a Mercedes-Benz convertible, and thanks to Immanuel's excellent negotiation skills she'd gotten a great deal on the sporty red car. She'd driven it home two days later, and every time Dionne looked at it she thought about Immanuel. He was a godsend, the kind of person who'd give a stranger the shirt off his back. Not a day went by that she didn't wish they were more than just friends.

"I better go," Immanuel said. "It's eight o'clock, and I still haven't made dinner."

"You should come over. The mushroom Bolognese is almost ready, and it smells divine." Dionne opened the jar of tomato sauce, poured it in the stainless steel pot and stirred slowly. "Should I set another plate at the kitchen table?"

"Can I eat in front of the TV?" he asked, his voice filled with amusement. "The home team is playing."

"I'll make an exception, but just this one time—" Hearing a noise behind her, she broke off speaking and glanced over her shoulder. The jar fell from her hands and shattered into a million pieces, sending shards of glass flying everywhere.

Her body was numb, paralyzed in fear, and a scream was trapped inside her throat. Narrowing her gaze, she zeroed in on the moving target. Someone was on her deck. The person was crouched down beside the table moving their hands in a wide sweeping motion, as if they were painting a picture. *What the hell?*

"Dionne, what's wrong? Are you okay?"

"S-s-someone's outside," she stammered, unable to believe what she was seeing. She rubbed her eyes, but the figure on her deck still remained. "He's on the patio."

"I'm on my way. Go upstairs and lock yourself in the bathroom," Immanuel instructed.

Her heart was racing erratically, but she spoke with confidence in a voice that masked her fears. "Hell no. This is *my* house, and I'm not going anywhere."

"I'm on my way. Call the police, and don't open the door unless you see a badge."

Dionne rejected his suggestion, didn't give it a second thought. "I can't call the police. I'm new to Brookhaven, and I don't want my neighbors to think I'm trouble."

"Forget about your public image and call for help."

"Immanuel, I have to go." Dionne hung up the phone and dropped it on the breakfast bar. Keeping her gaze on the back door, she moved over to the end table and rummaged around inside her purse. *Bingo!* Finding the can of Mace, she tiptoed to the back door and flipped on the patio lights. The stranger scrambled to his feet, jumped over the railing, and took off through the back yard. *Was he the only one? Was there someone else lying in wait?*

Deciding to investigate, she peered outside. She didn't see anyone. Spotting an aerosol can on the ground, Dionne unlocked the back door and stepped onto the patio. Her stomach muscles clenched, and dread flooded her body.

Dionne turned around and gasped. Cupping a hand over her mouth, she stared at the horrific image before her eyes. Expletives were sprayed on her house. Cruel, horrible words that pierced her soul like an arrow. *Who would do this? Why? What had she ever done to deserve being called a gold digger and a filthy whore?*

Hearing footsteps behind her, she whipped around, prepared to fight. She saw Immanuel running down the street and dropped her hands at her sides. Dionne felt a rush of emotion—gratitude, relief and an overwhelming sense of peace. Taking a deep breath steadied her nerves and stopped her legs from shaking. She had to be strong, had to keep it together, and willed herself not to cry.

"Dionne, what happened? Are you okay?"

"I'm fine," she lied, biting the inside of her cheek to ward off fresh tears. "He's gone. I scared him off when I turned on the outdoor lights."

Immanuel gave her a hug, held her tight, close to his chest. "Good thinking. I'm not surprised, though. You're as smart as they come."

His touch was warm and felt soft against her skin. Though it did nothing to soothe her troubled mind. Someone was after her, and she didn't know why. Was it Jules? A former employee with an ax to grind? Someone from her past she'd wronged?

"Go inside," he said, squeezing her shoulders. "I'm going to secure the property."

Dionne returned to the kitchen, saw the broken jar on the hardwood floor and grabbed her cleaning supplies from the broom closet. Her mind raced, jumping from one thought to the next as she swept and mopped. *Is Jules trying to hurt me? Is this retaliation for the divorce?*

Anger coursed through her veins. Dionne gripped the broom handle, imagined it was the perpetrator's neck, and decided she wasn't going down without a fight.

"Do you need any help?" Immanuel asked, quietly entering the room.

Dionne shook her head, emptied the dustpan in the garbage, and returned her supplies to the closet.

"Did you get a good look at the perpetrator?"

"No, it was too dark, and he was gone in the blink of an eye."

"It's not safe for you to stay here. That creep could come back."

She scoffed. She couldn't believe what she was hearing. "I'm not leaving my house."

"Yes, you are. Go upstairs and pack an overnight bag. You're staying with me."

"I won't let some sick bastard drive me away from my property."

"What if I book you the penthouse suite at the Hyatt?"

"I want to sleep in my own bed, in my own house, not at a downtown hotel."

His eyes narrowed, darkened a shade. "Are you always this stubborn?"

"Yes, as a matter of fact I am. I'm a Taurus, *and* Somali, and since you don't have a chance in hell of winning this argument you might as well quit while you're ahead!"

"Copycat." A grin claimed his mouth. "Can I at least take you out for dinner?"

"Not tonight. I'm tired, and I don't have the energy to make myself beautiful."

"You don't have to *make* yourself beautiful. You already are."

"Not in jeggings and an old T-shirt," Dionne said, gesturing at her casual clothes. "I feel my best when I'm all dolled up, and I wouldn't be caught dead wearing this in public."

"That's too bad. I like your look, especially your cute ponytail and bunny slippers."

And I love your smile.

Sniffing the air, he glanced around the kitchen. "What is that amazing smell?"

"Mushroom Bolognese. Do you want some?"

Flashing a devilish grin, he hungrily licked his lips and rubbed his flat stomach. "Heck yeah! You know I can't say no to food, especially homemade pasta. I'm Italian, and there's nothing I love more!"

Dirty dishes, empty wine bottles and bowls of junk food covered the wooden coffee table. Dionne and Immanuel were sitting in the living room, stretched out on the couch, watching the game on TV. The table was a mess, the kitchen, too, but Dionne was so full she couldn't move. She'd clean up later after Immanuel left, though she wouldn't mind if he spent the night. The thought excited her. Hours had passed since she'd scared off the vandal, but Dionne couldn't stop thinking about what had happened.

Her gaze fell across his face, sliding down his broad, muscled physique. He looked dreamy in his white ribbed shirt and loose-fitting pants, but it was the good-humored expression on his face that turned her on. He was telling her a story about the time he got lost with his brothers in Prague, and the sound of his hearty chuckles warmed her heart. "I'm glad you and Emilio are back on speaking terms. That's awesome."

"Yeah, it's cool. My grandmother's happy about it."

"Who knows? Maybe Emilio will ask you to be one of his groomsmen."

"I can't go to the wedding. I have to work."

"Work?" she repeated, incredulous. "But he's your brother. You should be there."

"I can't. Things are still tense between us, and I don't want to ruin Sharleen's big day."

"But…I was hoping you could show me around your hometown. There's so much to see and do in Venice, and I want you to be my tour guide."

"Don't worry. I have a big family. Someone will definitely step up to the plate."

Nodding, she masked her disappointment with a smile. "You're right. Emilio said Dante loves a good time, and he's already volunteered to show me around while I'm in town."

"Stay away from Dante," he warned. "Trouble follows him wherever he goes. I don't want you in harm's way."

Then come to Italy so we can be together, Dionne thought, wishing he weren't being so stubborn. Every time she thought about her trip to Venice she pictured herself with Immanuel—sightseeing, kissing and making love. Feeling her temperature rise, she pushed the thought away and dismissed his words with a flick of her hand. "You worry too much. I'll be fine."

"I have to. You're important to me."

"Then come to Venice," she said. "I want to see Italy through *your* eyes, not your brother's. And I don't want Dante's girlfriend to hate me for monopolizing his time."

"What girlfriend? My brother hasn't been serious about a girl since the third grade!"

Dionne laughed. "So, you'll attend Emilio and Sharleen's wedding?"

"I'll think about it."

His words gave her hope. "That's all I'm asking."

Chapter 13

It was midnight, and Dionne had to be at the office first thing tomorrow morning to meet with an eighties pop star struggling with depression. But instead of asking Immanuel to leave, she filled his empty wineglass with more Chardonnay, and turned up the volume on the stereo. They'd been talking for two hours, and the Sam Smith song playing in the background put her in a relaxed mood. Dionne couldn't remember the last time she'd felt this content, and although she was angry about the graffiti on her house, she refused to let it bring her down.

"Are you ready for your trip to Seattle?" he asked.

"I'm excited about the Leadership Conference, but I'm dreading the flight," she said, tucking her legs under her bottom. "Thank God for sleeping pills or I'd never travel."

"Have you finished your speech?"

"Yes, of course, and it's *really* good."

"I'm sure it is. You're an intelligent, articulate woman with a lot to offer. "

"You should come to the conference. It's a great networking opportunity, and I think you'll learn a lot."

"I'll get back to you. Let me check my schedule first, and see if I can free up some time."

Tasting her water, she watched Immanuel over the rim of her glass. A frown covered his face. He looked troubled, as if something was bothering him, and when he spoke, his voice was strained.

"Friday's the big day. How do you feel?"

Dionne raised an eyebrow. "I'm surprised you remembered."

"I remember everything that concerns you. You're my number one girl, remember?"

His words touched her heart, and a smile tickled the corners of her mouth. "I'm nervous about the meeting, but I'm trying to stay positive. Jules's attorney contacted us, so I'm hoping he's finally come to his senses and is ready to settle."

His expression was sympathetic, full of warmth and compassion.

"We've been arguing for months, and I'm sick of it. I just want it to be over so I can move on and start the next chapter of my life."

Immanuel picked up the remote control, pointed it at the stereo system and lowered the volume. "If you don't mind me asking, why has it taken almost a year to reach a settlement?"

"Because Jules wants to hurt me. That's all he cares about. I can't let him win."

Dionne surprised herself by opening up to Immanuel about her marriage, told him things she'd never told anyone, not even her sisters. He was easy to talk to, a sympathetic ear, and she was grateful he didn't judge her or minimize her feelings.

"Life doesn't get better by chance, it gets better by change, so don't be afraid to speak up for yourself," he advised. "Don't let Jules and his high-powered attorney dictate what's right for you, either. Your life is yours to create, and yours alone."

"I know, but Jules is fighting me at every turn. So is my family."

Immanuel squeezed her hand. "It's been a stressful year for everyone, hasn't it?"

Dionne swallowed hard, slowly nodded her head in agreement.

"Dante got divorced last year, and it took a toll on everyone, especially my nephew, but it was definitely for the best. There are some things you can't put a price on, like contentment and peace of mind. Dante's a lot happier now that it's just him and Matteo."

His words gave her pause, made her reflect on everything that had happened since she'd filed for divorce last year. Immanuel was right on. The divorce was stressing her out, always weighing heavily on her mind. Dionne couldn't go anywhere in her old neighborhood without people staring and whispering behind her back. She felt alone, as if no one were in her corner. She wanted to move on with her life, but how could she when Jules was being petty and vindictive?

"You have to outsmart him. Give Jules something he wants—" Immanuel answered the question she'd posed in her thoughts.

"You mean besides strippers?"

"What does he value more than anything? What does he hold dear?"

"His money, his privacy, his secrets…" An idea came to mind, and Dionne broke off speaking. She'd have to lie, and would need the help of one of her female employees to beat Jules at his own game, but it was worth a shot. Dionne was anxious for a fresh start, desperate to be free of Jules and his meddling, controlling family. If everything went according to plan, come Friday she'd be a free woman. "Immanuel, you're brilliant! I know what to do to win!"

He chuckled, then wore a lopsided smile. "I'm glad I could help."

"You're always helping me. It's like you're my good-luck charm or something."

Their eyes met, and the temperature in the room rose a hundred degrees. Sexual tension scented the air, filling the room with its sweet, intoxicating fragrance.

Dionne examined him thoroughly—his creamy olive skin, his piercing blue eyes, the intense expression on his face—and knew what he wanted, because she wanted the exact same thing. She craved him, desired him, had been dreaming of kissing him for weeks. Suddenly breathless, she waited impatiently for Immanuel to make the first move.

Seconds passed, then what felt like minutes.

Deciding to take matters into her own hands, she moved closer to him on the couch and gently caressed his soft, smooth skin with her fingertips. His scent overwhelmed her, increased her hunger. Dionne was shocked by the intensity of her feelings, how touching him made her body throb. He didn't speak. Didn't have to. The expression on his face said it all: he wanted her, too. No doubt about it.

Her heartbeat sped up; her pulse, too. Anxious to taste his lips, Dionne closed her eyes and slanted her head to the right. *He's going to kiss me! Finally! I thought this day would never come!* When nothing happened, she stared at him, baffled by his behavior. "What's wrong?"

"You're still legally married."

"I've been separated for months," she countered, her mind reeling from his words.

"In the eyes of the court you're still his wife, and I won't do something that's ethically and morally wrong."

Dionne felt her eyes widen and her lips part in surprise.

Why couldn't he be like other guys? Why did he have to do the *right thing*?

"I've been cheated on, and I'd never inflict that kind of pain on another human being."

Her skin burned with shame, and her body tensed. His rejection stung. It was so painful Dionne couldn't bring herself to look at him. *Now* she wanted to run and hide. Wanting to be alone, she stood and moved away from the couch. "You should go. It's late."

"Are you sure you don't want me to stay?" He sounded concerned, and wrinkles lined his smooth brow. "I don't mind, and I'll sleep better knowing you're safe."

"Immanuel, I don't need a babysitter. I can take care of myself."

"I know," he said with a knowing smile. "I've seen you in action."

Dionne opened the front door and stepped aside. "Get home safe."

"Thanks for dinner. Everything was delicious, especially the homemade bruschetta."

With a heavy heart, Dionne watched Immanuel put on his jacket and walk outside.

"Don't forget to put on the alarm before you go to bed."

"Don't worry, Dad. I won't."

He grinned, but Dionne didn't have the energy to return his smile.

"Workers from the Paint Doctor will be here first thing tomorrow to repaint the deck."

"Thanks for everything," she said. "I can always count on you to come to my rescue."

"That's what friends are for, right?"

Her shoulders sagged. *Friends? Is that* all *we are?*

"If you need anything just call. It doesn't matter how late."

Dionne couldn't get her lips to move, and nodded her

head in understanding. Her heart faltered when he kissed her on the cheek. Feeling light on her feet, she gripped the door handle to steady her balance. Her body was weak, desperate for him, but she exercised self-control, chose to stare at the hardwood floor instead of his juicy, sexy lips.

"Sleep well," he whispered, his soft, seductive voice arousing her needs. "And good luck on Friday. Remember what I said. Nothing is more important than your happiness."

He then jogged down the steps and disappeared into the darkness.

Chapter 14

The ninth-floor conference room in the Simmons & Sons Law Firm had vibrant oil paintings on the walls, eye-catching sculptures that beautified the glass shelves, and floor-to-ceiling windows that offered striking views of downtown Atlanta, but Dionne was bored out of her mind. Anxious to return to her office, she glanced at her watch for the second time in minutes. She was leaving for Seattle that evening, and she had a million things to do before her nine o'clock flight to Emerald City.

Folding her arms across her chest, she tapped her high-heeled shoes impatiently on the floor. Sunshine splashed through the windows, but it didn't improve her foul mood. Jules and his attorney were fifteen minutes late, and she had no choice but to wait. Dionne was sitting at the table with her attorney, a no-nonsense New Yorker by the name of Zakkiyah Givens. As she watched the seconds tick by on the wall clock, her anxiety increased.

Hearing footsteps outside the door, Dionne straightened

in her chair and adjusted her tweed suit jacket. She could hear male voices, someone speaking in a hushed whisper, and rolled her eyes to the ceiling. Jules and his attorney, no doubt. They were standing in the hallway, plotting her demise, but Dionne wasn't fazed. She had a plan A, B *and* C in her arsenal, and she wasn't leaving the prestigious law firm without a divorce.

Her cell phone buzzed, and she took it out of her purse. Dionne punched in her password, read her newest text message and smiled for the first time that morning. It was from Immanuel. His words of encouragement made her feel supported, cared for. He called every night to check up on her, but Dionne hadn't seen him since he'd left her house earlier that week. It felt longer than four days, more like four months, but after the conversation they'd had about her marital status she knew it was important to give him space. She thought about him constantly, wondered how he was doing, and hoped he was thinking about her, too. Doubtful, since women threw themselves at him 24/7, but they had a strong connection, and Dionne felt fortunate to have Immanuel in her life. That's why she'd planned a special surprise for him. After her meeting, she was picking him up from Mastermind Operations and treating him to lunch. Thanks to Immanuel, the painters had done a great job repainting her deck, and all traces of the graffiti were gone. Unfortunately, she was still getting prank calls on her cell phone. Dionne was considering changing her number, but decided she would talk to Immanuel about the situation first. He'd know what to do; he always did.

"Dionne, let me do the talking this time—"

"Absolutely not," she said, adamantly shaking her head. "I can speak for myself."

"Yes, I know, but the last time we met you threw your water glass at Jules. I don't want things to get out of hand again."

"He called me a bitch. What did you expect me to do?"

Pride brightened her eyes, covered her face.

"Let me handle Jules this time, okay? I do this for a living, and I eat creeps like him for breakfast!"

The door opened and Jules, and his attorney, a lanky man named Mr. Munson, marched inside. Dionne wrinkled her nose. The stench of nicotine and cologne was so heavy in the air her stomach churned. *What are they trying to do? Kill me? Is that their strategy?*

"Good morning," she said with a polite nod. "Let's get down to business, shall we?"

Mr. Munson set his briefcase on the table and flipped it open. "Mr. Fontaine has revised his initial offer, and I think you'll both agree it's more than fair. Here is a copy for your review."

He slid the document across the table, and Dionne read it carefully, ensuring she didn't miss anything. It was a sham. It was the same settlement agreement he'd offered her back in August. The only thing he'd changed was her home address. "I'm not signing this."

"I knew you'd come to your senses," Jules said with a toothy smile. Standing, he scooped his iPhone off the table with one hand, and straightened his gray double-breasted suit jacket with the other. "I'm going back to work. See you at home, babe."

"Don't call me that," she snapped, annoyed with his smug, cocksure attitude. "I'm not your babe."

His eyes narrowed, and his face hardened like stone. "You're not coming home?"

"Not a chance in hell."

Silence fell across the room.

"My client doesn't want to go to court," Mr. Munson said, clasping his hands together. "So what do we have to do to resolve this situation in a peaceful, amicable manner?"

Zakkiyah spoke up, but Dionne interrupted her. She had to. This was her life, and she wanted to speak for herself. "I want sole ownership of the land I bought in Somalia last year," she said in a firm voice. "I bought it with my own money, as a gift to my parents, and—"

"Anything purchased during our marriage is joint property, babe. You know that."

"Mr. Fontaine is right. In order to keep the land, you'll have to offer him a financial settlement, or you can sell the property and split the proceeds evenly down the middle."

Jules sneered in triumph, as if he'd beat her at a game of chess. He draped an arm over the side of his chair. His eyes were filled with arrogance and hate.

Her temperature rose, and perspiration clung to her skin. Dionne could hear her heart beating, the loud, pulsing sound throbbing in her ears. She wanted to hurt Jules, imagined herself kicking him in the shin with her high-heeled shoes, but logic prevailed and she abandoned the thought. It was a challenge, but she remained calm and didn't lunge across the table to smack the grin off his face.

Glancing discreetly at her diamond Cartier watch, she watched the seconds tick by with nervous anticipation. Five…four…three…two…one…

Jules's cell phone rang at precisely ten o'clock, and he put it to his ear. "Talk to me," he chirped, drumming his fingers on the table. "I'm sorry, what did you say your name was?"

"Don't let Jules rattle you," Zakkiyah whispered. "Stick to the game plan…"

"No comment." Jules ended the call and rounded on Dionne, shouting and screaming insults. Sweat dripped down his face, and the veins in his forehead throbbed. "You're a real piece of work," he said, speaking through clenched teeth. "When were you going to tell me about your exclusive interview with *Atlanta Tribune* magazine at one o'clock today?"

Dionne made her eyes wide, pretended she was confused by the question. She hated his tone and his dark, malevolent stare. He looked like the villain in a horror movie, and seemed to transform right before her eyes. To win, she had to project confidence, not fear, so she held her head high and met his steely gaze. "I don't know what you're talking about."

"Yes, you do!" Jules gestured to his cell phone, raising it high in the air. "That was the editor of *Atlanta Tribune*. She asked if I wanted to be interviewed for the magazine as well."

Dionne remained quiet, crossed her legs, and pretended to study her manicured nails.

"This is how you repay me? After everything I've done for you?" Jules slammed his fist on the table and surged to his feet. He raged like a tropical storm crashing into dry land, yelling, cursing, screaming obscenities. "Dammit, Ross, don't just sit there! Do something!"

"There is nothing we can do," he answered with a shrug of his shoulders. "It's a free world. We can't stop her from doing interviews."

"Then I'll sue her ass for defamation of character." Eagerly nodding his head, he stuck out his chest and rested his hands on his hips. "You're not the self-made woman you claim to be. You're a fraud. Nothing but a low-down dirty gold digger who married up."

Dionne held a finger in the air. "Call me out of my name *one* more time and I'll spill the beans about your yearly sex trips to Thailand."

His jaw dropped, and the color drained from his face.

"That's right, Jules, I know all about your overseas 'business trips,'" she said, making air quotes with her hands. "I met with your former secretary last night, and she was most helpful."

"I can't believe this shit," he grumbled. "You stupid, conniving bitch."

"A bitch would have told *everyone* about your penchant for screwing underage girls, but I didn't say a word. I'm saving that juicy tidbit for my media tour."

His face crumpled like a sheet of paper. "You have no proof."

"Tune in to my weekly podcast tomorrow. It's going to be a fascinating hour, and I think you'll be impressed with how resourceful I am."

Jules dropped into his chair and tugged at the knot in his tie. "What do you want?"

He sounded defeated, looked it, too, but Dionne wasn't fooled by his woe-is-me act. He was trying to gain sympathy by playing the victim, tricking her so he could get the upper hand. He'd done it before, too many times to count, over the course of their tumultuous five-year marriage. If given the chance he would do it again.

"I want the land I bought in Somalia and a million dollars for my shares in Fontaine Enterprises, and the Pathways Center expansion project must be completed by March of next year."

He furrowed his eyebrow. "That's it? That's all you want?"

Zakkiyah clutched Dionne's arm. "Ask for spousal support and attorney fees," she whispered, dollar signs twinkling in her dark brown eyes. "That's another two million."

"This isn't about money."

"Of course it is! He's worth millions, and it's time to make him pay up."

"If I accept spousal support, Jules will hold it over my head for the rest of my life. Besides, I have my own money. I don't need his."

Mr. Munson cleared his throat. "Do we have a deal?"

Dionne wanted to jump for joy, but she remained in her seat. "Yes."

"Fine, I'll draft the papers and fax them to your attorney's office first thing tomorrow."

Zakkiyah opened her briefcase. "I have the revised divorce agreement right here."

Jules and Mr. Munson shared a bewildered look.

"Go ahead," she urged, pushing the document across the table. "Take a look."

"We'll need a few days to look it over."

Dionne shook her head. "You have an hour."

"An hour!" He was breathing heavily, huffing and puffing like a sprinter at the end of the hundred-yard dash. His eyes were wide with alarm. "We need more time."

"You've had almost a year. Enough is enough." Dionne rose to her feet, picked up her purse and put on her vintage-style sunglasses. "It's your choice. You can sign the divorce decree, or I can head to the *Tribune* for my one o'clock interview. What will it be?"

Dionne opened her car door and collapsed onto the driver's seat. It was over. Finally. After months of countless arguments and disagreements, she was a free woman. Free of Jules, his lies and his meddlesome family. Her plan had worked, gone off without a hitch, and she had Annabelle Clark to thank. She'd asked the novice life coach to call Jules posing as a magazine reporter, and she had given an award-winning performance.

Her thoughts turned to her family. Dionne wondered what they would say when she told them the news. Her parents were going to be upset—her sisters, too—but for once she wasn't concerned about their happiness. They didn't know what it was like living with Jules, had no idea how selfish and insensitive he could be, and Dionne knew in her heart she'd made the right decision. She'd done what was best for her, and that was all that mattered.

Starting the car, Dionne was surprised to see the time on the dashboard clock. It had taken Jules and Mr. Munson fifteen minutes to read the divorce decree, but they'd wasted another hour arguing with Zakkiyah about the confidentiality agreement. There was no media tour in the works, no interviews lined up with local magazines or reporters. But she'd signed the necessary papers and laughed to herself when Jules sauntered out of the room like a champion.

Dionne put on her seat belt and slowly backed out of her parking space. If she hurried, she could make it to Mastermind Operations by noon. Immanuel loved the food at the Italian bistro across the street from his office, and he'd treated her to lunch at the cozy family-owned restaurant on several occasions. *The last time we were there was the first time we almost kissed,* she thought with a dreamy sigh. Just the thought of it aroused her, made her giddy with excitement. Immanuel had been a great friend to her the past couple months, and if not for his great advice, she'd probably still be at Simmons & Sons Law Firm arguing with Jules. Dionne couldn't wait to share her good news with Immanuel and took off like a rocket down the block.

An hour later, Dionne pulled up in front of Mario's Italian Restaurant. She glanced at the front window to see if the restaurant was busy, and her lips parted in surprise. Dr. Pelayo was sitting at a round table, and she wasn't alone. Immanuel was her date. At the sight of him, her heart ached. He looked gorgeous in his casual business attire, more handsome than she remembered. *Is that even possible? I* just *saw him a few days ago!*

Dionne examined her competition, assessed the emergency room doctor with a critical eye. Her makeup was flawless, her dark brown hair was a mass of lush curls, and her crimson dress served up an eyeful of cleavage. More shocking still, she had love in her eyes. Dr. Pelayo was glowing, wearing a radiant smile. Her expression was the picture of happiness.

Dionne felt like a Peeping Tom and knew she should leave, but she couldn't stop staring at the attractive couple. Their attraction was evident, their chemistry so strong and intense she could feel the electricity pulsing between them from a hundred feet away. Dionne wanted to go inside and confront them, but struck the idea from her mind. Immanuel wasn't her boyfriend. Hell, they'd never even kissed. If she stormed into the restaurant, he'd think she was a nut. Her feelings were hurt, but she had to let him be. Had to back off. He was interested in someone else, and she had no choice but to accept it.

Sadness filled her, made her heart throb and ache. Immanuel was dating Dr. Pelayo. That was the real reason he'd rejected her the other night. Her marital status had nothing to do with it. *Why didn't he tell her the truth? Did he think she couldn't handle it? Or was that his way of letting her down easy?*

Dionne sat there thinking about the events of the past few weeks and the time she'd spent with Immanuel. They were some of the happiest moments of her life. Dining at premier restaurants, exploring museums and art galleries, hanging out with his family, spending hours on the phone confiding in each other. He'd come to mean a lot to her, and seeing him with another woman was a painful, crushing blow.

Dionne pressed her eyes shut and drew a deep breath to calm her nerves. She didn't have time to fret about Immanuel and his new girlfriend. She had work to do, lots of it, before Sharleen dropped her off at the airport. Nothing was worth missing her flight.

Taking one last look at the couple, Dionne stepped on the gas and pulled into traffic.

Chapter 15

The mood inside the grand ballroom at the Sheraton Seattle Hotel was lively and upbeat. Dionne couldn't wait to get on stage and deliver her speech to the sold-out crowd. Participants wearing smiles and name tags wandered around the room checking out the various booths and displays. Being among distinguished executives at the helm of profitable companies made Dionne realize this was the "big break" she'd been waiting for her whole life.

Boisterous laughter and conversation filled the bright, spacious room. As Dionne walked around, greeting people and shaking hands, thoughts of Immanuel filled her mind. *I wish he were here. We would have had fun together.*

Arriving in Seattle late last night, she'd headed straight to the hotel. Sophisticated and stylish, it was one of the city's flashiest, most popular hotels. It was a prime location for shopping and sightseeing, and its trendy restaurants were a hit among tourists and locals alike. The establishment had everything a traveler could want, and

Dionne planned to take full advantage of all the amenities the hotel had to offer.

Upon arriving at her suite, she'd collapsed onto the king-size bed. Instead of going to sleep, she'd turned on her laptop. She wanted her speech to be perfect, something that inspired and incited change, and had stayed up for hours working on it.

That morning, after a light breakfast, she'd enjoyed an in-suite massage, then a bubble bath. Immanuel had phoned while she was getting dressed, but she'd let his call go to voice mail. He didn't leave a message, and she didn't call him back. *What for? So he could gush about his new-found love?* Dionne didn't want to hear it. So instead of fretting about a man she wanted—but could never have—she enjoyed some retail therapy at her favorite department store. Feeling generous, she'd bought Chanel scarves for her mom and sisters, toys for her nieces and nephews, and a wool fedora for her dad to add to his enormous hat collection. Hopefully the gifts would help smooth things over with her family, and they'd forgive her for not being the perfect daughter and sister they wanted her to be.

"Dionne, how wonderful to see you again!" The program coordinator, a slender woman with bone-straight hair and wide hips, touched her forearm and led her to the stage.

Standing behind the lectern, Dionne watched as participants hurried to their seats. Sweat drenched her palms, and her mouth dried. To calm her nerves, she took a deep breath and allowed the fragrant scent in the air to relax her mind. Over the years, she'd spoken at workshops and career day events at prestigious universities, but this was her biggest stage yet, and Dionne didn't want to mess up.

"Please give a warm welcome to life coach and best-selling author Dionne Fontaine."

Polite applause filled the air, and cell phone cameras flashed.

Holding her head high, she straightened her shoulders and strode confidently across the stage. Dionne took her place behind the lectern, opened her leather-bound notebook and greeted the crowd with a wide smile. "I'm thrilled to be here, and I want to thank committee organizers for giving me the opportunity to speak to you about my personal journey to success."

The back door opened, and Dionne's gaze landed on the new arrival. Her eyebrows shot up, and her skin burned like fire. *Immanuel?* Feeling unsteady on her feet, as if her knees would buckle, she gripped the lectern stand to steady her balance. *What is he doing here? How did he know where to find me? Is he alone, or is his girlfriend with him?*

Her gaze zeroed in on his lips—the thick, juicy lips she was dying to kiss—then slid down his chest. Immanuel always looked amazingly cool, like a badass action hero in a Hollywood movie. Seeing him made her heart swoon. His camel-brown coat and black dress pants fit Immanuel perfectly, and his stare was intense, so laser-sharp she couldn't take her eyes off him. Dionne heard someone gasp, then watched as people turned around one by one to look at the back door. Eyes popped, jaws dropped, and women old enough to be his mother licked their lips and fanned their faces as if they were suffering from heatstroke.

Realizing she was ogling him, Dionne snapped to attention and glanced down at her notebook. Taking a moment to review her notes reminded her what was at stake. Dionne didn't have time to make eyes at Immanuel. She had forty-five minutes to deliver her message. She couldn't afford to squander a second of her time.

To capture the attention of everyone in the room, she raised her voice and spoke directly into the microphone. "As a woman of color, born to an immigrant couple from Somalia, I've experienced racism, sexism and discrimination, but I made a conscious decision to grab hold of my dreams. Through hard work and determination, I built a life that I'm proud of." Dionne waited until she had everyone's attention before she continued speaking. "I'm living the American dream, and it has nothing to do with where I live, how big my house is, or how much money I have in the bank…"

Dionne felt on top of the world, in complete control. She spoke openly, didn't hold back, and her transparency paid off. Everyone was staring at her, and the room was so quiet she could hear her pulse pounding in her ears.

"As employers and entrepreneurs, it's up to us to make things better for the next generation following in our footsteps. We—" Dionne emphasized the word as her gaze swept over the crowd "—we have to fight for fair treatment for all. I'm calling on each and every one of you to join the good fight, because equality doesn't just benefit women and visible minorities. It benefits *everyone*…"

Participants straightened in their seats, furiously taking notes, emphatically nodding their heads. Dionne spotted Immanuel snapping pictures of her with his iPhone and frowned. His baby blues were bright, filled with excitement, and he looked proud.

"Live your passion," she advised. "Do what brings you joy, whether that's teaching, photography or microbiology. Do it to the best of your ability."

Dionne didn't want to stop, wished she could spend the rest of the day imparting the words of wisdom her parents had shared with her over the years, but when she glimpsed her watch, she knew she had to wrap up her speech. "I hope your dreams are fully realized, and that you leave your mark on the world. Thank you for your time. It's been a pleasure speaking to you."

The crowd broke into applause, whistled and cheered with more zeal than baseball fans. Participants jumped to their feet, clapped so long and so loud, her heart swelled with happiness. Feeling like a rock star, Dionne took a seat on one of the padded chairs behind the lectern and expelled a deep breath. She spotted Immanuel watching her and returned his smile. Then she remembered his cozy lunch date with Dr. Pelayo yesterday and looked away.

The rest of the afternoon flew by. Each speaker was witty and entertaining, and by the time the conference wrapped up at three o'clock, Dionne was bursting with new ideas to build her brand and improve staff relations at Pathways Center.

Dionne stepped off the stage and shook hands with conference organizers. She was tired and her feet ached, but she signed copies of her latest life-coaching book, *90 Days to a Better You*, handed out business cards and posed for dozens of pictures.

Eager to speak to Immanuel, Dionne searched the room for him. She found him standing beside one of the food tables, and as usual he wasn't alone. Women were approaching him left, right and center, but when their eyes met he shouldered his way through the crowd and headed straight toward her.

Her heart jumped in her throat. To mask her inner turmoil, Dionne wore a blank expression on her face and arched her shoulders. His cologne fell over her, making it hard to think, but she forced her lips to move and greeted him warmly. "Hi. How are you?"

Immanuel wrapped his arms around her. "Baby, I'm so proud of you!"

Baby? The word reverberated around her mind, and when he kissed her cheeks and lovingly stroked her shoulders, Dionne thought her heart would burst with love. *Love?* The word scared her, conjured up painful memories, but she couldn't deny her feelings for Immanuel. He was every woman's dream, and she loved spending time with him. But that didn't mean she was willing to be his side chick. Pulling out of his arms, she swallowed hard and adjusted her cropped blazer and checkered dress.

"Dionne, your speech was outstanding! You killed it up there!"

"I did?" she asked, stunned by his praise. "You really think so?"

"Isn't it obvious? You got a standing ovation, and your fans mobbed you when you left the stage." He wore a broad smile. "I didn't think I'd ever get my turn with you."

"Immanuel, what are you doing here? You're supposed to be in Atlanta."

"You invited me, remember?"

Dionne frowned. "I did?"

"Yeah, when we were watching the game."

"I was joking. I didn't think you'd actually come."

"Do you want me to leave?" he asked in a solemn tone.

"Does your girlfriend know you're here with me?"

Wrinkles creased his forehead, and a scowl crimped his lips. "What girlfriend?"

"I saw you at Mario's with Dr. Pelayo yesterday, and it was obvious you guys were having a good time." Dionne searched his face for signs of deception, noting every move he made, but he seemed genuinely confused. Still, she asked the question weighing on her mind. "How long have you been a couple?"

"We're not."

"But she likes you."

Immanuel took Dionne's arm and led her to a quiet corner, away from the crowd. "Elena and I are not dating. I met with her yesterday to discuss a business matter, not to make a love connection. And besides, I'm interested in someone else."

Dionne arched an eyebrow, giving him a skeptical look.

She didn't know what to think. Was he feeding her a line or telling the truth? How could she know for sure?

"How did things go at the law firm yesterday?"

"We signed the divorce decree," she answered with a sad smile.

Immanuel rested a hand on her shoulders. "How do you feel?"

"Relieved, tired and anxious to get on with my life."

"If you don't have plans tonight I'd love to take you out for dinner."

"Can I take a rain check? I'm beat, and I want to turn in early tonight."

"Let's meet in the lobby at seven o'clock. That will give you plenty of time to rest."

"Are you *sure* you're not dating Dr. Pelayo?" she asked, unable to shake her doubts. In her experience, men like Immanuel didn't have one girlfriend, they had several, and Dionne didn't want to be his flavor of the week. "You guys have great chemistry and it's obvious she likes you—"

"Dammit, Dionne, I'm not attracted to her. I'm attracted to *you*."

Immanuel lowered his head and crushed his lips to her mouth. The kiss stole her breath and every lucid thought in her mind. She was stunned by his brazen behavior, but she didn't pull away. His kiss was exhilarating, and Dionne was hungry for more. She wanted him, craved him, and wasn't letting go of him until she had her fill. *Is this actually happening? Are we kissing or am I daydreaming?*

The kiss was definitely worth the wait. His lips were warm and tasted sweeter than chocolate. Dionne was under Immanuel's spell, caught in a sensuous, erotic trance she couldn't break free from. It was heaven. A perfect, incredible first kiss, and she didn't want it to ever end. Blocking out the noises around them, she linked her arms around his neck and caressed the back of his head with her hands.

"That was one hell of a kiss."

Dionne opened her eyes and met his piercing blue gaze. The ballroom was quiet, filled with only a handful of people, but to her surprise everyone was staring at them.

"Are we on for dinner tonight?"

"After *that* kiss?" she asked, making her eyes big and wide. "Absolutely!"

Releasing a hearty chuckle, he pulled her even closer to his chest. Immanuel nibbled on her bottom lip, then kissed her hard on the mouth with urgency. His behavior was reckless, nothing short of criminal, and she loved every minute of it. His passionate kiss, his caress, the naughty X-rated words he whispered in her ear. Immanuel was dreamy in every sense of the word, and feeling his hands on her body made her wish they were alone in her suite instead of in the grand ballroom. "You're gorgeous," he praised, nuzzling his chin against her neck. "And you smell delicious."

"I know, *and* I taste good, too."

"Let me be the judge of that."

He gave her another slow, sensuous kiss and she groaned into his mouth.

"I'll walk you back to your room," he said smoothly, caressing her hips.

Immanuel escorted Dionne out of the ballroom and through the hotel lobby.

I can't wait for dinner, she thought as they boarded the crowded elevator, hand in hand. He drew his hands down her arms, stroked her hips, and Dionne felt the urge to jump into his arms and kiss him all over. *Seven o'clock can't come soon enough!*

Chapter 16

Immanuel knocked on suite 1014 and waited patiently for Dionne to answer the door. Seconds passed with no sight of her. Where was she? Had she changed her mind about having dinner with him? Was she out with another man? One of the businessmen she'd met at the conference that afternoon? Immanuel rejected the thought. Dionne wouldn't stand him up. Not after that scorching, red-hot, goodbye-for-now kiss they'd shared outside her suite earlier. It was even better than their first, more passionate and intense. He'd never experienced anything like it before and was hungry for more. If not for a housekeeper interrupting them, they'd still be in the hallway making out.

Immanuel's cell phone rang, and he fished it out of his jacket pocket. His shoulders tensed, and his blood ran cold. He had nothing to say to Jules and wished the CFO would lose his phone number. *Doesn't he have a company to run?* Tired of Jules's incessant phone calls, he let the call go to voice mail.

Immanuel remembered their last conversation vividly. Last week, he'd had his report delivered to Jules via UPS, and the CFO had called him screaming bloody murder. Instead of taking responsibility for the mistakes he'd made in his marriage, he'd blamed Immanuel for "losing" his divorce, and threatened to ruin his security business. Jules was a sore loser, a bully who threw a fit whenever he didn't get his way, and Immanuel had no respect for him.

Immanuel wasn't fazed, didn't give a damn what Jules thought. He'd written a thorough report, and he was proud of the work he'd done. There was no proof of Dionne's infidelity, no evidence that she'd ever cheated, and he wasn't going to frame her to win favor with Jules. His grandmother had raised him to be honest and trustworthy, and he wasn't changing for anyone—not even one of the wealthiest men in the state. Now that his business relationship with Jules was over, he could pursue Dionne with a clear conscience. She was a beautiful soul with a big heart, and he'd do anything for her. To keep her safe, he'd commissioned his best employee to follow her 24/7, and although nothing else had happened since the graffiti incident, he'd implored his staff to stay on high alert.

His thoughts returned to their last time together. As Immanuel was running to Dionne's house, he'd spotted a black Cadillac idling at the end of the street and paused to read the license plate number. He'd asked Malcolm to help him track down the car and driver, and was confident the trail would lead straight to Jules Fontaine.

Immanuel didn't care what it took; he was going to keep Dionne safe. He worked long hours and looked forward to spending his downtime with her. They had a lot in common, and they never ran out of things to discuss. Immanuel wanted a life partner, someone he connected with on every level, and Dionne appealed to him in every way. She was the kind of woman he could bring home to his family, someone he'd be proud to have on his arm. Immanuel was scared of being hurt again, but he was ready to take a chance on love once more.

Immanuel knocked on the door again, longer and louder this time. A terrifying thought stabbed his heart with fear. Was Dionne in trouble? Was that why she wasn't answering the door? Because she was in danger? Taking a deep breath, he told himself to remain calm. He was overreacting. He'd only been waiting a couple of minutes. There was no need to panic.

He sent Dionne a text message, then knocked again. Hearing a noise behind him, he glanced over his shoulder and watched a group of housekeepers exit the elevator. Immanuel recognized one of the women from that afternoon and greeted her in Italian. He told her he'd locked himself out of his room, and asked if she'd be kind enough to open the door for him.

A frown darkened her face. "I'm sorry, sir, but that's against hotel policy."

To persuade her, Immanuel opened his wallet, took out a hundred-dollar bill, and put the money in her hands. "Please?" he asked, glancing at his watch. "I'm going to an important business dinner, and I don't want to be late."

Seconds later, Immanuel entered suite 1014 and flicked on the lights. "Dionne?" Sliding his cell phone into his pocket, he noticed everything was in its rightful place. Colorful cushions decorated ivory chairs, potted plants filled the air with a refreshing scent, pendant lights gave the suite a touch of class, and oversize windows revealed picture-perfect views of Seattle.

"Hello? Dionne? Are you here?" he called, walking into the master bedroom. Relief flooded his body, and released a deep sigh that fell from his lips. Dionne was sleeping. His eyes widened, as did his mouth. Her purple satin robe kissed her thighs, and her hair fell in curls around her shoulders. He stood in the doorway staring at her, thankful that she was safe and sound.

His gaze slipped down her curves, and his heart galloped. Immanuel recognized he was losing it and took a moment to regroup. Taking a deep breath didn't help. His heart continued to race, and he couldn't take his eyes off her juicy, sensuous mouth. God help him. Coming inside her suite was a bad idea, but his legs wouldn't move.

It amazed Immanuel how small she looked on the king-size bed. He was used to seeing her all dolled up, but preferred her simple, natural style. She didn't have any makeup on, and she smelled like tropical fruit, not a cosmetics counter.

His temperature soared. His inner voice told him to turn around and head for the door, but the urge to caress and stroke her smooth brown skin was overwhelming. Moved by the needs of his flesh, he took off his jacket, chucked it on the end of the bed, and kicked off his shoes. Immanuel knew he was tripping big-time, but his desires were all-consuming.

Stretching out on the bed beside her, he slid an arm around her waist. Their bodies were a perfect fit. Dionne didn't stir, but Immanuel was in heaven. He was holding Dionne, and it was a great feeling.

"This is a pleasant surprise." Dionne rolled onto her side and faced him. Opening her eyes, she fluttered her long, thick lashes. "I heard your voice, but I thought I was dreaming."

"I'm sorry. I didn't mean to wake you. I got worried when you didn't answer the door, so I asked one of the housekeepers to let me inside your room. I hope that was okay."

"Sorry about that. I called my mom, and after we got off the phone I dozed off."

"How is your mother doing?"

Sadness flickered across her face and seeped into her voice. "Miserable. I told her about the divorce, and she scolded me for being a disobedient daughter. Aside from that she's great," Dionne said, with false enthusiasm. "Thanksgiving is her favorite holiday, so she's busy getting ready for next week."

"Why are your parents so upset about the divorce? Couples split up every day," he pointed out. "Hell, my father's been divorced so many times I've lost count!"

"Divorce is shameful in the Somali culture, and the fact that I've been divorced twice is a huge embarrassment for my family. My failures cast a negative light on my parents, and I feel guilty for not living up to their expectations."

"Join the club. I was supposed to follow in my father's footsteps and become a championship race car driver, but I couldn't cut it."

"Was your dad disappointed in you?"

"That's the understatement of the year. He cut ties with me when I joined the Italian military, and said I tarnished the Morretti name and image by becoming a soldier."

"But the military is such an honorable and worthy profession."

"Tell that to my old man."

"What's your relationship like with your father today?"

"Strained. We rarely talk, but I make a point of seeing him whenever I'm in Italy. Even if I just stop by his villa to see my siblings for a short period of time. My stepsisters and -brothers are teenagers, and it's important to me to be a part of their lives."

Immanuel heard his cell ring, knew it was Malcolm calling from the distinctive ringtone, but he didn't move. His friends wanted him to meet up with them in Las Vegas to watch a boxing match at the MGM Grand tomorrow night, but he wasn't leaving Dionne.

"Your cell phone's ringing," she said, peering over his shoulder. "It's on the end table."

"What cell phone? I don't hear anything."

He reached out and touched her hair, curling a lock around his index finger.

"Do you still miss your fiancée?"

The question caught him off guard, but he answered truthfully, telling Dionne everything that was in his heart. "No, not anymore. I met a smart, captivating beauty with one hell of a right hook, and she's the total package," he said, his eyes glued to her face. "Seeing her is the best part of my day, and I hate when we're apart."

Her eyes smiled. "She sounds like an amazing woman. You should keep her."

"I plan to."

"This is nice. Lying in bed talking with you. We should do this more often."

Immanuel drew his hand across her cheek, and she purred in his ear. "Can I kiss you?"

A grin shaped her mouth. "Please do."

Immanuel nipped at her bottom lip, licking it with the tip of his tongue, and Dionne thought she'd die in anticipation. Desperate for him, she crushed her mouth to his. His lips were soft, the best thing she'd ever tasted. She wanted to be kissed, to be held and loved, and relished being in his arms. Her body ached for him, yearned for his touch.

Seizing his hands, she guided them to her hips, moved them down her thighs and over her bottom. That was all the encouragement Immanuel needed. He untied her robe, tossed it to the floor, and lowered his face to her breasts. He pushed them together, flicking his tongue against her erect nipples. He lavished them with kisses, sucked them into his mouth, stroking, massaging and caressing them. His touch fueled her desire. Immanuel grabbed her butt, squeezed it as if it were a Georgia peach and he was desperate for a bite.

"Your ass is amazing."

"Your *hands* are amazing," she gushed, her words falling from her lips in a breathless pant. She couldn't help thinking about her past relationships, and realized this was the first time she'd ever initiated sex with a lover. Immanuel excited her, made her experience feelings she'd never felt before, and Dionne wanted to show him how much he meant to her. She kissed him, parted his lips with her tongue, then flicked it against his. Pleasure filled her, coursed through her quivering body. "I could stay here with you, like this, for the rest of the night."

"That can be arranged. We can have room service in bed."

"*Or* we can feast on each other."

"I love how you think."

And I love you. Dionne held her tongue. To prevent herself from confessing her feelings, she slammed her mouth shut. "I want to make love tonight."

"To me?"

"No, to the hotel bellman," she teased, snuggling against him. "Yes, you. You're the only man I need."

"Making love is a big step."

"I know, but I'm ready. Aren't you?"

"Baby, I want you, but it's too soon."

Too soon? Are you kidding me? I've been dreaming about this moment for months!

"How would it look if I put the moves on you the day after your divorce is finalized?"

Rolling her eyes, she pulled out of his arms and swung her feet over the side of the bed. "Forget I said anything," she snapped, annoyed that he'd rejected her yet again. "I'm not in the mood to play games. I'm going to get dressed—"

"Come here. You're not going anywhere."

Immanuel grabbed her hand and dragged her down on top of him. He smothered her face with kisses, and she shrieked in laughter. "Do you have any idea how much I want you?"

"No. Show me."

Roughly cupping her breasts in his hands, he lowered his mouth and circled her nipple with his tongue. He sucked it, licked it, bit it softly with his teeth. He played in her hair, grabbing fistfuls, stroking her body as if his sole purpose in life were to please her. And she loved it. His kiss, his touch, the feel of his hard, muscled physique against hers. For weeks, she'd been lusting after him, and tonight she was going to have him—over and over and over again.

"I've been lying to myself for weeks," he whispered, his gaze as dreamy as his seductive tone. "I convinced myself you weren't my type, that we were all wrong for each other. But you're the only one for me, and I want you for more than one night."

His confession stunned her, and she fumbled with her words. "What are you saying?"

He answered with a deep, passionate kiss that gave her chills all over. He took off his clothes and chucked them on the floor. They lay naked in bed, exploring each other's bodies, kissing, laughing and talking dirty. Feeling his mouth on her neck, her breasts and her navel caused quivers to ripple across her skin. Dionne loved how broad and muscular his shoulders were, and couldn't resist kissing, squeezing and licking them.

Immanuel crushed his lips against hers. Dionne moaned into his mouth, took everything he gave, still wanting more, needing more. She loved kissing him, couldn't get enough, and wondered what the rest of his body tasted like. To find out, she licked from his ears to his chest and abs, then sucked his erection into her mouth.

Pleasure sparked in his eyes. Dionne twirled her tongue around his length and eagerly sucked, licked and kissed it. Having Immanuel inside her mouth made her feel strong, invincible and powerful. She'd never felt more comfortable in her skin and wanted to please Immanuel more than anything. Dionne couldn't get enough of him, and the more she stroked and caressed his hard, muscled body, the more she wanted him.

Immanuel opened his wallet, took out a condom and ripped open the packet. Watching him excited her, made her mouth wet with hunger. It was finally going to happen. After weeks of flirting and "accidentally" touching, she was finally going to experience the pleasure of having him inside her. Aroused and anxious, she felt blood rush to her core.

Immanuel brought her to his side, kissed her hard on the lips, and rolled the condom over his shaft. Dionne hungrily licked her lips. His erection doubled in size, right before her eyes, and she parted her legs to welcome him inside.

Immanuel slid his erection against her clit, slowly, as if he wanted to torture her. Tingles danced down her spine, erupting across her flesh. Dionne tried to keep it together, to hold her emotions in, but moans of satisfaction streamed from her lips. His movements were slow, deliberate, and each kiss increased her desire. She couldn't believe what he was doing to her, and he wasn't even inside her yet.

Immanuel gripped her hips, then eased his erection inside her. It was a snug fit, so damn tight she felt every inch of his length. Dionne couldn't stop shaking and lost complete control of her limbs. She was in her hotel suite, having the best sex of her life, but her mind was in the clouds, off in another stratosphere, no longer connected to her body.

"I love being with you, Dionne. You're perfect in every way…"

Soaking in his words, she reveled in his praise and admiration. It had never been like this before. They moved in perfect sync, holding each other tight. To stifle the wild, fevered noises streaming from her mouth, Dionne buried her face in the pillow. Immanuel picked it up and tossed it on the floor.

"Don't do that," he growled. "I want to hear every sound you make, every erotic moan."

Their lovemaking was fast and furious, an intense burst of adrenaline. It was the most thrilling hour of her life. He kissed her with a savage intensity, took everything she gave and more. Like his kiss, his stroke drove her wild. His erection swelled inside her, filling her sex. Immanuel was an incredible lover, the best she'd ever had, and she'd never forget their first time together.

Wrapping her legs around his waist, she grabbed his butt and pulled him even deeper inside her. Lightning struck Dionne's body. An orgasm stole her breath, made her wild with delirium. Immanuel gathered her in his arms and held her to his chest. He pumped his hips, moving at a fast, frenzied pace. His head fell back, and he groaned as he climaxed. Breathing heavily, he collapsed onto the bed and drew her to his side.

Seconds passed before her mind cleared and her feet touched the ground. Her skin was drenched in sweat, burning hot, but Dionne rested her head on his chest and closed her eyes. Immanuel pulled her closer to him and held her close. His arms were home, a warm, safe place. For the first time in years she felt an overwhelming sense of peace. *Wow, I can't believe that just happened. It was wonderful, amazing, beyond my wildest dreams!*

He stroked her hair, neck and shoulders, whispering sweet words into her ear. "I'm glad you invited me to Seattle," he said, pressing a kiss to her forehead. "I have an incredible weekend planned for us, and a big surprise for you on Monday morning."

"Immanuel, I'm leaving for Atlanta tomorrow."

"Change your flight and spend a few more days with me."

"I can't—"

"You can't, or you won't?" Immanuel cupped her chin in his hand and raised an eyebrow. "What's the point of being the boss if you can't break the rules sometimes?"

"I have a meeting on Monday morning with Channel 6 that I can't afford to miss."

"What's the meeting about?"

"The station did a story on me back in May, and I hit it off with the head producer," she explained, unable to contain her excitement. "He's developing a new reality show called *Celebrities Gone Wild*, and he wants me to be the resident life coach."

"Really? You'd agree to let cameras follow you around twenty-four/seven?"

"Absolutely. I want to help people in need of guidance and support, and television would be a great platform to show why life coaches are vital to society."

"When would you have time to do a TV show?" He stared down at her with a concerned expression on his face. "You already work eighty hours a week."

"I'll make time. This deal could catapult Pathways Center to the top, and I'll do anything to make my business more successful."

His frown deepened, but he spoke to her in a soft, soothing voice. "Since we only have twenty-four hours together, we better make the most of it."

"I agree. Seattle is one of my favorite cities in the world, and I'm up for anything."

"Do you want to order in, or go out? I made reserva-

tions at the best French restaurant in the city, but I'm cool
with staying in if that's what you wa̅nt—"

"I don't want food. I want to make love again."

His eyebrows shot up.

"I hope you're ready for round two, because I'm *starv-
ing*." Her gaze slid down his chest; her hands, too. Just as
she had suspected, his erection was rock hard. *Lucky me!*
she thought, rising from the bed. Feeling his eyes on her,
she sashayed across the room, switched her hips to arouse
and entice him. "I'm going to take a shower." Pausing in
the doorway, she tossed a seductive look over her shoulder. "Are you coming?"

Chapter 17

Eagles soared in the clear blue sky, and the sun was the size of a beach ball—the most brilliant and radiant thing Dionne had ever seen. The 360-degree views of the city were spectacular, but nothing beat being with Immanuel. Standing on the observation deck of the Seattle Space Needle kissing him was the perfect way to end their romantic dream date. Seattle had lush landscapes, take-your-breathaway architecture and some of the best restaurants on the West Coast. Dionne loved everything about the charming, sophisticated city.

Snuggling against him, Dionne reflected on the past twenty-four hours. He'd loved her all night, made her body sing in every position imaginable, and now she had a permanent smile on her face. That morning, after making love in the shower, they'd dressed and enjoyed a hearty breakfast in the hotel restaurant. They'd spent the afternoon wandering around Pike Place Market, touring the Theo Chocolate Factory and admiring Italian Renaissance paintings at the Seattle Art Museum. As they strolled along the crowded streets, they'd snapped selfies at famous landmarks. The city had everything a traveler could want—culture, history, entertainment—and Immanuel had made sure she'd experienced a bit of everything. He'd promised to bring her back to Seattle for the Venetian ball, and Dionne was looking forward to returning for the black-tie event in February.

"You're addictive," he said, his words a hungry growl. "I can't get enough."

Dionne tightened her hold around his waist and sighed inwardly when he brushed his lips against her mouth for the second time in minutes. In his arms she felt safe, protected, and after everything that had happened the past few weeks his embrace was welcome.

"Do you want to grab a bite at Chico Madrid before we head to the airport?"

Dionne groaned and rested a hand on her stomach. "No way. I'm stuffed."

After a quick stop at the hotel to change, they'd taken a cab to SkyCity, the revolving restaurant in the Space Needle. It was the place to see and be seen in Seattle, and there was no shortage of bling in the dining room. Sitting cozy in their booth, they'd feasted on seafood, Peking duck and Italian wine. Feeding Immanuel chocolate cheesecake, Dionne had marveled at how much their relationship had changed since their first date. Six weeks ago, she was nervous about being alone with him, and now she wanted to spend all of her free time with him. Dionne was so comfortable with him, she confided in him about her problems. During dinner, she'd opened up to him about her struggles at work, her failed marriages, and her strained relationship with her parents and sisters.

Wrapped up in each other's arms, they boarded the elevator and got off in the lobby. Outside, locals streamed in and out of trendy restaurants, street performers sang and danced, and laughter spilled out of nearby bars and cafés. The air smelled of salt water, a clean, refreshing scent that made Dionne remember the romantic boat cruise Immanuel had taken her on last night. For hours they'd talked, danced and kissed. Their personalities complemented each other, but it was their differences that kept things exciting and interesting.

On Sixth Avenue, Dionne searched the streets for a taxi. "I don't see a cab anywhere."

"Let's walk. It stopped raining, and now it's a gorgeous autumn night."

Wrinkling her nose, she stared down at her designer outfit. Her gold ankle-tie pumps complemented her black leather dress perfectly, but they weren't made for an evening stroll. To please Immanuel, she'd straightened her hair and put on a sexy outfit and sultry makeup. He'd been complimenting her all night, and when he wasn't praising her look, he was stealing kisses and stroking her hips. "The hotel is six blocks away," she pointed out, glancing up and down the block for a yellow cab. "I don't know if I can walk that far in these heels."

"I'll carry you if you get tired."

"Save your energy for later." Dionne winked. "You're going to need it."

Strolling down the street, they chatted about their favorite places in Seattle, their plans for Thanksgiving and her upcoming trip to Italy. "I want you to be my date for Sharleen and Emilio's wedding." Dionne held her breath, waited anxiously for his response, but he didn't speak. "Please? I hate flying, and I need you to keep me company."

"No, you don't. You pop a sleeping pill and it knocks you out, remember?"

Dionne wanted to kick herself, wishing she hadn't told him about her fear of flying. She thought for a moment.

"It's a ten-hour flight. Imagine how much fun we'll have in first class."

"Baby, I'm sorry. I can't."

"But Italy's home. Don't you want to see your friends and family—"

"It's not home. Not anymore. I can never live in Venice again, and I don't want to."

"Never?" Her ears perked up, and her feet slowed. "Why not? What happened?"

"It's a long story."

"We have time." Dionne led him over to a wooden bench and sat down. "Our flight doesn't leave until six. That gives us plenty of time to talk."

He didn't move, so she patted the space beside her. "Please?"

Nodding his head, he took a seat and clasped his hands in front of him. He spoke in a whisper, as if each word was a struggle. "I left Venice because I was receiving death threats."

"Death threats!" Her pulse quickened, and her heart thumped in her ears. Dionne heard her cell phone ringing inside her purse, but she ignored it and blocked out the noises on the busy downtown street. She wanted to hear his story, so she leaned forward and moved closer to him on the bench. His scent aroused her, teasing her senses, but she kept her hands in her lap and off his chest. "Immanuel, what happened?"

"I provided security for the ambassador to the US for several years."

His voice was so low Dionne strained to hear what he was saying.

"It was an open secret that the ambassador had affairs, and one night while I was doing my rounds, his wife propositioned me to get even with her philandering husband."

"What did you do?"

"I turned her down, but she told her husband I approached her for sex. My colleague, a man I treated like a brother, corroborated her story." His eyes narrowed, and a dark shadow crossed his face. "I was arrested, charged, and spent a night in jail."

"That's ridiculous! You did nothing wrong, and there was no proof!"

"The charges were eventually dropped, but the damage had already been done. My business and reputation were tarnished. I had no choice but to leave town."

Resting a hand on his back, she slowly rubbed his neck and shoulders. It killed her to see him in pain, and Dionne wished there was something she could do to make things better. "Is that why you left Venice? Because of the stress of the investigation?"

Immanuel lowered his gaze to the ground. "I was receiving death threats, my office was vandalized numerous times, and I couldn't go anywhere without someone calling me a rapist."

"Baby, that's awful."

"Needless to say, the ordeal taught me a valuable lesson about life. The only person I trust is myself. Not my friends, not my family, and certainly not a girlfriend or colleague—"

"Immanuel, that's not true." Dionne touched his cheek and waited for him to look at her before she continued. "You can count on me. I'm not going anywhere. You have my word."

He nodded his head, but his frown remained.

"I'm glad you relocated to Atlanta, Immanuel. It was a *very* smart move."

"I agree. My business is taking off, I've reconnected with my relatives here in the States, and best of all I met you." Immanuel caressed her cheek, drew his thumb down her nose and across her lips. "You're an incredible woman, and I feel fortunate to know you."

"I'm the fortunate one." Dionne stood, sat down on his lap and draped her arms around his neck. She'd never felt more connected to anyone, and wondered if they could have a strong, lasting relationship. He protected her, cared for her, and she wanted Immanuel for more than just a night. "You saved my life, and I'm forever in your debt."

His expression softened, and his hold tightened around her waist. His baby blues were irresistible, and so was his smile. Dionne lowered her mouth and tasted his lips. Lust shot through her veins, ricocheted through her body. He caressed her arms and neck, playfully brushing his nose against hers. She didn't have the courage to tell Immanuel what was in her heart, so she communicated her feelings with her lips.

"I wanted to tell you sooner about my past, but I didn't know how," he confessed, breaking off the kiss. "I was embarrassed about what happened with the ambassador's wife, and I thought if I told you the truth you'd want nothing to do with me."

Dionne held his gaze. "You thought wrong."

"I'm glad I did."

A family of five with two rambunctious toddlers walked by, and Immanuel stared at them. Dionne saw the longing in his eyes, his sad smile, and wondered what was on his mind. "Would you like to have a family of your own one day?"

"If you had asked me that question five years ago, I would have laughed out loud, but I've had a change of heart. My cousins, Demetri, Nicco and Rafael, have all married beautiful, successful women, and I get jealous whenever I'm around them." Immanuel took her hands in his, holding them tight in his grasp. "What about you? Would you ever consider getting remarried?"

"Immanuel, I've been divorced twice."

"What does that have to do with anything? Your past doesn't dictate your future."

"I'm unlucky in love, and after two failed marriages I realize it's just not for me," she answered with a shrug. "That's why I'm going to focus on my business and building my brand."

"You're being too hard on yourself. You're an incredible woman and any man would be proud to call you his wife." Immanuel kissed the tip of her nose and ran his fingers through her hair. "I know I would."

Her skin prickled from his touch. He slid his tongue inside her mouth, swirled it around, and she pressed her body against his. Caught up in the moment, she yielded to the needs of her flesh, kissed him until she was hot, breathless and dizzy. "Think we have time for a quickie before our flight?" she asked, stroking the back of his neck.

Immanuel squeezed her thighs. "Baby, we'll *make* time."

Chapter 18

"I had a great time with you this weekend." Immanuel picked up Dionne's hand, raised it to his mouth and kissed her palm. "When you get back from Venice, I'm taking you to this quaint and cozy bed-and-breakfast in Savannah. It's ridiculously beautiful. Just like you."

His words made her feel sad and excited at the same time. *If you want to spend time with me, then come to Italy!* Sharleen and Emilio's wedding was in two weeks, but despite her best efforts, Immanuel was dead set against attending the three-day celebration. "I'd love that," she said, gazing into his deep blue eyes. "It sounds romantic."

"We're going to have the time of our lives," he promised.

They were standing in the airport parking garage, leaning against the hood of Immanuel's sports car, and Dionne couldn't wait until they got to her house so that they could make love. "Immanuel, I don't care where we go or what we do, as long as we are together."

He kissed her then with incredible tenderness, and she melted into his arms. His lips were her weakness, so potent her ears tingled and her thoughts scattered. He held her tight, as if he was desperate for her, and lovingly stroked her skin. Immanuel was confident, refined and sophisticated. And he wanted her. It was a heady feeling, one that filled her with pride and boosted her confidence. He was always teaching her things, treated her with warmth, kindness and respect. When they were together nothing else mattered.

A car horn beeped, breaking the spell, and Immanuel ended the kiss. He helped Dionne inside the car, jogged around to the driver's-side door, and got in. Immanuel put on his seat belt, and then started the engine. Stepping on the gas, he sped through the parking garage and exited Hartsfield-Jackson Atlanta airport.

Dionne had napped during the flight from Seattle, and now she was wide-awake and ready to hang out with her man. The words echoed in her mind. *My man! I love the sound of that,* she thought, admiring his handsome profile. *And I love the way he makes me feel. He is, without a doubt, the sweetest man I've ever met, and he'll always be my hero.*

"You're spending the night at my place."

His hand climbed up her thigh, tickled her skin, and Dionne giggled.

"I'll drive you to the TV station in the morning, and pick you up when you're done. We'll have lunch, then play hooky for the rest of the day. Sound like a plan?"

"You don't even have to ask. I'd love to."

Ten minutes later, they arrived in Brookhaven and stopped at the local grocery store. Immanuel bought snacks, wine and a movie, but Dionne doubted they'd end up watching the new romantic comedy. They'd had a quickie in her hotel suite before heading for the airport, but Dionne wasn't satisfied. If anything their lovemaking left her wanting more. Desperate for him, she couldn't wait to get him out of his clothes and into her bed. The thought aroused her, and a grin overwhelmed her mouth. "Can we stop at my place on the way to your house?" she asked, opening her Gucci handbag in search of her house keys. "I need to grab something to wear for tomorrow, but it won't take long."

"Of course, baby. Anything for you."

Immanuel flashed his trademark grin, a smile so dreamy it made her heart dance.

"Keep talking like *that* and I may never leave your house."

"Works for me. I love the idea of coming home to you every night."

Dionne was shocked, but she didn't let her feelings show. The thought of setting up house with Immanuel, a man she'd known for not even a couple months, should have terrified her, but it didn't. Last night, after making love, they'd had an emotional heart-to-heart talk. Immanuel made her feel so safe and secure, Dionne wanted to be with him forever.

Immanuel parked in the driveway and got out of the car. He opened the trunk, grabbed her overnight bag and wrapped an arm around her waist. Dionne loved that he was always kissing and touching her, and couldn't wait to get him inside her house.

"Your house in complete darkness," he said. "You should have left some lights on."

"Sorry, Dad, I forgot."

Immanuel slapped her bottom. "That's Big Daddy to you."

Dionne screamed in laughter. She liked their playful banter and enjoyed kidding around with him. Immanuel was protective of her and overreacted at times, but she didn't mind.

"I'll go inside and secure the property." Immanuel took the keys from her hands and pecked her cheek. "You wait here."

"Whatever you say, Big Daddy!"

His eyes twinkled, and his shoulders shook when he laughed. Immanuel unlocked the front door, flipped on the lights in the foyer, and slid inside the house. Dionne poked her head in the doorway, watched as he disabled the alarm and checked the living room windows. He told her to stay put, then jogged upstairs to the second floor.

Hearing tires screech on the road, Dionne glanced over her shoulder. Her eyes narrowed, and her body stiffened. The white Jaguar with the tinted windows parked at the curb belonged to Jules. She had to get rid of her ex before Immanuel returned. She didn't want him to ruin their night, and shuddered to think what would happen if the two men came face-to-face.

Jules jumped out of the driver's seat and slammed his door so hard Dionne was surprised the window didn't shatter into a million pieces. Her pulse pounded in her ears as she marched down the walkway. "Jules, you're not welcome here. Please leave."

"You must think I'm stupid—"

"You're right, I do," she mumbled, folding her arms across her chest. He smelled of whiskey and was slurring his words. Jules shouldn't be talking, let alone driving, and Dionne wondered if she should call the police to take him home.

"I heard about your interview at Channel 6 tomorrow morning," he said, shouting his words. "Cancel it, or I'll sue your ass for defamation."

Dionne glared at him. Jules liked to think he was the Almighty, but he wasn't, and she was sick of him telling her what to do. "The meeting has nothing to do with you."

"That's not what my sources tell me."

"They're wrong."

It was a struggle to keep her temper in check, but she didn't lash out at him. There was no telling who was watching. "If you don't leave right now I'll call the police and have you arrested for trespassing." Dionne took her cell phone out of her jacket pocket. "Don't tempt me—"

"Baby, is everything okay?"

Dionne heard Immanuel's voice behind her and summoned a smile. She glanced over her shoulder to reassure him everything was okay. Then all hell broke loose. Jules rushed past her, pushed Immanuel in the chest, and swung wild, frenzied punches that didn't connect.

"You no-good son of a bitch! I told you to trail her, not screw her!" Baring his teeth, he shouted insults and threats. "You're finished in this town. You hear me, Morretti? Done. I'm going to ruin you if it's the last thing I do."

Dionne couldn't catch her breath, fought to get oxygen into her lungs. It felt as if an orange was stuck in the back of her throat, and her temples throbbed in pain. *I told you to trail her, not screw her!* The words blared in her eardrum, piercing her heart and soul.

"Don't listen to him," Immanuel said, his tone filled with urgency and desperation. "He's trying to break us up, but I won't let that happen. Dionne, we belong together, and—"

"Is it true? Did he hire you to…" Dionne lost her voice and broke off speaking.

"Of course it's true," Jules snapped, his tone laced with hate. "I've paid him thousands of dollars since August, and I have the documentation to prove it."

"Jules hired me to trail you, but it's not as sinister as he's making it sound."

Her stomach heaved. The truth hit her hard, like a crippling blow to the chest. Dionne stared at Immanuel, noted his lowered gaze and bent shoulders, and knew he was lying to her. She couldn't believe this was the same man who'd promised to protect her, who had just made love to her hours earlier. He'd been conspiring with Jules for months, and his betrayal cut like a knife. Immanuel wasn't a hero; he was a fraud. His bitter betrayal broke her heart.

A sob rose in her throat, and it took everything in her not to burst into tears. Dionne willed herself not to cry. She was determined to keep it together in the presence of her adversaries. She felt dumb for trusting Immanuel— her ex-husband's hired hand—and her pain was so great her body ached. He'd played kickball with her heart, filled her head with empty lies and promises, and Dionne had no one to blame but herself.

"This isn't over, Morretti." Jules rounded on Dionne and spoke through clenched teeth. "No one messes with me and gets away with it. Cancel that interview at Channel 6 or else."

Immanuel stepped forward and jabbed a finger at Jules chest. "If you even *think* of hurting her I'll hunt you down and beat you like the dog you are."

"Don't touch me. This suit costs more than your entire wardrobe…"

Anger roared through Dionne's veins, and her hands balled into fists. She wanted to smack them both—especially Immanuel for deceiving her—but she kept a cool head.

"We'll see who gets the last laugh, Morretti."

Jules stalked over to his car, jumped inside and took off down the street.

"Baby, let's go inside."

"So, you can lie to me again? Hell no."

"We need to talk—"

Dionne cut him off. "About what? How you plotted with Jules to destroy me?"

"Don't say things like that."

"Why not? It's the truth." Something triggered in her brain, and she gave a bitter laugh. "Is Immanuel even your real name, or is that a lie, too? For all I know, you're married with kids. You're an accomplished liar, so I wouldn't put it past you."

"Dionne, don't talk like that. You know me—"

"No, I don't. You and Jules are cut from the same cloth. I wish I'd never met you."

"Don't let him come between us. He's not worth it."

"There is no us. We had sex a few times. That's all it was."

A cold wind whipped through the air, and Dionne hugged her arms to her chest. There was nothing left to say. They were over, and there was nothing he could say to change her mind. Dionne spun around, but Immanuel caught her arm.

"Don't touch me," she snapped breaking free of his grasp. "Don't you dare touch me!"

"Ma'am, is everything okay?" A jogger in an Adidas sweat suit and neon green sneakers stood on the sidewalk. "Is this guy bothering you? Do you want me to call the cops?"

Too choked up to speak, Dionne rushed inside the house and locked the front door behind her. There, in the privacy of her home, she curled up on the couch and let the tears flow from her eyes.

Chapter 19

Immanuel felt like the scum of the earth, and not just because he'd lied to Malcolm about being sick for the fourth consecutive day. He'd hurt Dionne—the only woman he'd ever truly loved and given his heart to. He was mad at himself for causing her such pain. It had been almost a week since their argument, but he still couldn't get her words out of his mind.

Hanging his head, he closed his eyes and raked his hands through his hair. *What was I thinking? Why didn't I tell her the truth when I had the chance?* He'd tried coming clean on numerous occasions, but he always lost the nerve. He didn't know what to say. It was never the right time. Or at least that's what he had told himself whenever guilt troubled his conscience. The truth was he didn't tell Dionne about his relationship with Jules because he didn't want to lose her. His wait-and-see approach had backfired, and now she wouldn't talk to him.

Immanuel walked into the living room, fell into his

favorite chair and reached for the bottle of vodka on the side table. *When did I finish it?* he wondered, scratching his head. *Last night? Two days ago? On Sunday when I was looking at pictures of Dionne on my cell phone?* He longed to see her, and would give anything to hold her one more time. He'd gone to Pathways Center so many times the receptionist had threatened to call the cops on him. Thankfully, Sharleen had come to his aid. She'd promised to talk to Dionne on his behalf and texted him words of encouragement every day. Not that it helped. Immanuel was miserable, sick over what he'd done. He had called her every single day and had gifts delivered to her office, but to no avail. His heart and mind were at war with each other, and for the first time in his life he didn't know what to do. Immanuel wanted a wife, not a playmate, and the only woman he wanted was Dionne. He craved her, longed to touch her and replayed the intimate moments they'd shared over and over again in his mind. In bed, she'd unleashed her wild side, given him the best sex of his life. A week later he could still hear her moans of pleasure in his ears.

His gaze drifted to the window. The dark, overcast sky mirrored his bleak mood. Living without Dionne was excruciating. Last night, after talking with Sharleen, he'd gone to Dionne's house to apologize. Her car was parked in the driveway and the lights were on in the kitchen, but she didn't answer the door. She was always on his mind, and he wanted her more than anything. He'd screwed things up, and now he had to fix them, but how?

Immanuel's cell phone rang, and he swiped it off the coffee table. Every time his phone rang he prayed it was Dionne, but it never was. Today was no different.

"Malcolm, what do you want?"

"I love you, too," he teased with a dry laugh. "I found Brad McClendon."

He gripped his cell, pressing it closer to his ear. Troubled about what Jules had told him weeks earlier, Immanuel had done extensive background checks on all of Dionne's past and present employees. There had been no red flags, nothing to raise alarms, but he'd been unable to locate her former right-hand man.

"After leaving Pathways Center, he reunited with his estranged wife, relocated to Augusta, and started his own life coaching business."

"If Brad didn't attack Dionne, then who did?" Pacing the length of the room, he voiced his frustrations. "Damn, after all these weeks of hard work, we're back to square one."

"Not so fast, Immanuel. There's more. I tracked down the guy who rented the Cadillac Escalade you saw parked on Dionne's street the night her house was vandalized."

"Good work, man. Where is he?"

"At Friendship House. It's a homeless shelter on Williams Street."

His ears perked up. In Seattle, he'd spent long hours talking with Dionne about her family, her career and her volunteer work. It was during that conversation at a downtown coffee shop that he'd learned about her charity work at Friendship House. The Fontaine Family had been involved with the organization for decades. Over the years Dionne had done everything including teaching cooking classes, tutoring students in math and feeding homeless youth.

"He's an ex-con with a lengthy rap sheet," Malcolm explained.

"I knew it. Jules paid him to attack Dionne, and now we finally have the evidence to prove it."

"You're wrong. It wasn't her ex."

Immanuel frowned. "Are you sure?"

"Positive. Jules doesn't know the guy, but someone in his family does, and you'll never believe who it is. I've been a PI for two decades, but even I didn't see this coming…"

Stroking his chin, he listened closely to what his friend had to say. Finally, after weeks of chasing leads and dead ends, all the pieces of the puzzle fit. Anger burned inside him, roared through his veins. He wanted to get even with the person who'd orchestrated the attack on Dionne, but he governed his temper.

"Do you know where Friendship House is?"

"No, but I'll find it. See you in twenty minutes."

Ending the call, he pocketed his cell and grabbed his car keys off the kitchen counter. Ready to even the score, he stalked through the living room and into the garage. Immanuel knew who was after Dionne, and they were going down.

"Get out or I'll throw you out!"

The velocity of Jules's tone made the windows in the thirteenth-floor conference room shake, but Immanuel didn't move. Tucking the manila envelope under his arm, he locked the door and folded his arms across his chest. Now he had everyone's attention. He was at Fontaine Enterprises on official business, not to shoot the breeze with the first family of Atlanta. He wasn't leaving until he confronted the person who'd been terrorizing Dionne for weeks.

His heart ached as an image of her flashed in his mind, but he pushed past his pain and swallowed the lump in his throat. After he left Fontaine Enterprises, he was going to find Dionne, and this time he wasn't leaving Pathways Center until they spoke. He didn't want to talk to her at work with her staff listening in, but what choice did he have? He'd given her space, but enough was enough. It was time to bring his baby home. He wasn't going to lose her, not after everything they'd been through, and he was desperate to reconcile with her.

"I'm calling security." Jules snatched the phone off the cradle and dialed.

"Good idea. They can arrest the person who's been terrorizing Dionne."

"Who are you?" Mrs. Fontaine asked, clutching her necklace. "What do you want?"

Seated around the glass table were Jules, his older sister, Adeline, and his parents, Francois and Helene Fontaine. They were all smartly dressed, and wore matching frowns.

"That's Immanuel Morretti, Dionne's new boy toy," Adeline said, her tone dripping with disgust. "You should be ashamed of yourself for carrying on with a married woman."

"And *you* should be ashamed of yourself for hiring a hit man."

The phone dropped from Jules's hand and fell to the table. "What?"

"Adeline, what is he talking about?" Mr. Fontaine asked. "What's going on?"

Immanuel stared at Adeline. Her eyes were dark, and her expression was blank. "Guess who I tracked down at Friendship House? Your old buddy Tyler Keaton. I wonder what your country club friends would think if they knew you socialized with hardened criminals."

The room sweltered with heat, and the air became thicker than fog.

"You have no proof," Adeline said with a dismissive shrug. "It's your word against mine, and who do you think the police are going to believe? A woman with a stellar reputation, or a lowly security guard with a chip on his shoulder?"

Immanuel opened the envelope, took out Malcolm's report, and dropped it on the table. "It's all right there. You were mad at Dionne for filing for divorce, so you hired Tyler to attack her. You rented him a car and gave him hundreds of dollars' worth of gifts and cash."

"Adeline! No!" yelled Mrs. Fontaine. "You didn't!"

"Ma, I had to do something. I couldn't let Dionne tarnish our image."

Jules spoke through clenched teeth. "I told you I could handle it."

"Jules, please. You talk a good game, but you're a spineless jellyfish."

Sweat dripped down Mr. Fontaine's face. "Are you going to tell the police what you know?" he asked, his eyes wide with fear. "Surely we can work something out that's beneficial for all parties involved."

"I bought your buddy Tyler a one-way ticket back to Detroit, and I personally put him on the bus." Immanuel addressed Adeline. "If Dionne so much as breaks a nail, I'll tell the police everything I know, so stay the hell away from her."

Adeline wouldn't meet his gaze, looking everywhere but at him.

Turning toward the door, he remembered a conversation he'd had with Dionne weeks earlier about her charity work and spun back around. "Adeline, since you like helping ex-cons, you're going to make a million-dollar donation to Re-entry Project Inc. on Dionne's behalf." He added, "And you're going to do it by four o'clock today."

"A million dollars!" Mrs. Fontaine shrieked. "That's blackmail!"

"No," he said in a firm tone of voice. "That's justice."

Immanuel stalked out of the room and marched down the hall.

"Morretti, wait up!"

Stopping, he faced Jules. He'd been wrong about the CFO. Jules had a vicious temper and an ego the size of

Texas, but he wasn't the one bent on revenge; his older sister was.

"I like the way you work, Morretti, and I could use someone with your insight and initiative at Fontaine Enterprises. Can we set up a time next week to talk?"

Immanuel didn't know if Jules was serious or pulling his leg, but it didn't matter. Dionne was his priority, not working with Fontaine Enterprises, and he didn't want to do anything to jeopardize their relationship. "No, thanks. I have my own business to run."

Jules released a deep sigh, shuffling and shifting his feet. "Tell Dionne I'm sorry. I had nothing to do with her attack. I feel horrible about what my sister did to her," he said in a low voice. He released a deep sigh. "If I could go back in time I would. Dionne's a good woman, but I took her for granted…"

I know, and if she takes me back I'll never, ever do the same.

"Take care of her, okay? She deserves happiness, and I hope she finds it in you."

Minutes later, Immanuel exited the elevator and marched through the sun-drenched lobby. He called Dionne's cell phone, and when her voice mail came on he left another message—his third one that day. Immanuel didn't know what else to do. He'd texted Sharleen and discovered Dionne had the day off work. At this rate, he wouldn't see her before she left for Italy on Friday. He had forty-eight hours to reconcile with her, but Immanuel feared he would run out of time. Feeling discouraged, he searched his contact list, found the number he was looking for and waited anxiously for the call to connect.

"Immanuel? What's up?"

He yanked open his car door and dropped into the driver's seat. "Emilio, I messed up."

"You sound like crap. What's going on?"

Immanuel vented, told his brother about his argument with Dionne and their bitter breakup last Sunday night. "I feel like I'm losing my mind," he confessed, staring aimlessly out the window. "Dionne won't speak to me, and I'm dying a slow death without her."

"You guys were a no-show for Thanksgiving, so I knew something was wrong," Emilio said quietly. "Dwelling on the past isn't going to help matters. We need a plan."

"We? You're going to help even though we have a strained relationship?"

"Had," he corrected, emphasizing the word. "Let's start over. What do you say?"

"I'd like that." A smile found his lips. "My baby was right. You *are* a good guy."

They laughed, and for the first time in days Immanuel felt hopeful about his future. He had Emilio back and a new, improved attitude. All he needed now was the woman he loved to make his life complete. "You're leaving for Venice on Friday, right?"

"Yeah, we have to arrive a few days before the wedding to finish up paperwork."

"Is Dionne traveling with the bridal party?"

"Yeah, she'll be on my private plane. Why?"

Immanuel shared his thoughts with his brother. Fired up, he felt his shoulders straighten and a rush of adrenaline that bolstered his confidence. He wanted Dionne back more than anything in the world, and wanted to prove his love in a big way. "What do you think?"

"That's your plan?" Emilio asked quizzically. "No offense, bro, but it stinks."

"Do you have a better one?"

"Yeah, I do. I don't mean to brag—"

"Then, don't. Just help me make things right with Dionne."

"To win her back, you'll have to fly to Italy."

Sweat clung to his shirt, made his palms damp and cold. Immanuel didn't know if he could. It was too soon. *What if the locals turned on him while he was out sightseeing with Dionne? What would she think of him? Would his past inevitably destroy their future?*

"Bro, the clock is ticking. What's it going to be? Do you want Dionne back, or not?"

Chapter 20

The words *Venice Skies* were painted on the side of the jet. The white custom-made airplane reeked of wealth and sophistication. It was a hotel in the sky, as luxurious as a penthouse suite, and filled with the best furnishings money could buy.

Stepping inside the bright, spacious cabin, Dionne noted the milk-white interior, plush seats and designer tables, and the state-of-the art electronics. R&B music played on the mounted speakers, and Dionne was surprised to see dozens of people chatting, eating and dancing as if they were at a nightclub. Stewards dressed in crisp navy blue uniforms served appetizers, poured champagne and walked around offering guests cashmere blankets.

"Good morning, Dionne. How are you?" Emilio kissed her on each cheek. "You look incredible. Is it just me or does she get more beautiful each day?"

Sharleen nodded her head and gave Dionne a one-armed hug. She looked adorable in her flashy bride-to-be getup, and her diamond tiara sparkled in the sunlight streaming through the cabin windows. "Girl, I love your outfit. You should be on an Italian runway!"

As if, she thought, rolling her eyes behind the protection of her sunglasses. *I haven't slept in days, and I have a killer headache. But you're my girl, and I want to support you on your big day.*

Waving at the members of the bridal party, Dionne strode through the cabin and found a seat at the rear of the plane, away from the raucous, inebriated group. She wanted to sleep, not socialize, and hoped Emilio and Sharleen's friends and family would keep their distance.

"Champagne?"

It was 9:00 a.m., far too early to have some bubbly, but Dionne could use something to quiet her mind and settle her nerves. Smiling her thanks, she accepted the flute and took a long drink. The liquid flowed down her throat, instantly calming her. A pleasant scent inundated the air, and her mouth watered at the aroma. Silver food trays filled with pastries, gourmet cheese and heart-shaped fruit covered the tables. Dionne didn't have the energy to get up. It had been a long, stressful week, and she was looking forward to resting during the ten-hour flight.

Kicking off her high heels, she rested back in her seat. Her thoughts returned to Thanksgiving. Upset with Immanuel, she'd decided to spend the holiday with her family, instead of at Emilio's Greensboro estate. After dinner, she'd had a frank talk with her parents and sisters, and they'd all promised to stop meddling in her life. Dionne didn't believe them, but she was glad everything was out in the open and they'd finally cleared the air. The highlight of the day had been playing flag football in the backyard with her nieces and nephews. Running around with the kids had helped take her mind off Immanuel.

Dionne opened her purse, took out her cell phone and

stared at the screen. The picture had been taken at Pike Place Market, and looking at the image of Immanuel made her miss him. Her nose twitched and her vision blurred, but she maintained her composure. Dropping her phone, she picked up her bottle of sleeping pills and flipped it open.

"Is everything okay? You seem upset, you're so quiet and withdrawn." Sharleen sat in the empty seat across from Dionne, put her purple feather boa over her shoulders and wore a sympathetic smile. "Talk to me, Dionne. I want to help."

"I'm great, fine, couldn't be better." It was a lie, one she'd been repeating for the past several days, but she'd suffer in silence rather than burden her friend with her problems. "Don't worry about me. Worry about memorizing your vows, because you're getting married in forty-eight hours!"

Sharleen pointed at the blue pill bottle. "What's that?"

"Sleeping pills. Can't fly without them."

"Sleeping pills!" Scowling, she plucked the bottle out of Dionne's hand and furiously shook her head. "You can't go to sleep. We're going to play party games, and I want you to mingle with our friends and family. It's a wedding celebration, remember?"

"I *knew* I should have flown commercial," Dionne grumbled, wondering if it was too late to de-board the plane. Peering down the aisle, she noticed the cabin door was locked and cursed under her breath. "I'll socialize *after* my nap."

"Why are you so tired? You were off yesterday and the day before."

Dionne swallowed a yawn. She hadn't had a good night's sleep since breaking up with Immanuel, and their argument had dominated her thoughts for weeks. He phoned constantly, sent her emails, text messages and dozens of red roses. Dionne wasn't impressed. Like most men, Immanuel thought flowers and expensive gifts could fix everything. He was fooling himself if he thought material things would win her over.

He'd shown up at her office, begging to see her, but Dionne couldn't bring herself to go to the reception area to talk to him. Not yet. Her emotions were still raw, her heart heavy with despair, and every time she remembered his bitter deception, tears filled her eyes.

"Let's compromise. I'll sleep for an hour, then join the festivities."

Sharleen leaned over and touched her leg. "Have you talked to Immanuel?"

"No. And I don't plan to. We're over." Her voice was quiet, filled with such anguish she didn't recognize it. Her eyes were moist, but she didn't cry. Dionne didn't want to ruin the festive mood inside the cabin or upset the glowing bride on the eve of her fairy-tale wedding. "Our relationship was built on lies and deception, and I have nothing to say to him."

"Dionne, don't say that. Immanuel loves you."

"No, he doesn't. He's been plotting behind my back from day one—"

"You have every right to be upset, but don't let your anger cloud your judgment."

Dionne took issue with what Sharleen said, but she didn't argue. *Was it true? Was she blinded by hurt and anger? Should she try to work things out with Immanuel?*

"Love is when your partner's happiness is more important than your own, and from day one Immanuel has done everything in his power to protect you. There's nothing he wouldn't do for you, and he's always had your best interests in heart."

"Then why did he deceive me? Why did he make me look like a fool in front of Jules?"

"I don't know. You'll have to ask him."

*I can't. I'm emotional and upset, and every time I think
about what he did I cry.*

"The next time you see Immanuel, let him explain.
Don't interrupt. Just listen."

Dionne nodded, realizing her friend had given her great
advice. On Tuesday, when she returned from Italy, she'd
meet with Immanuel. It was time. Time to move on and
put the past behind her. She didn't know if their relationship could be salvaged, but she wanted to know the truth
once and for all. "When did you get so wise?"

"When I met my Emilio." Her gaze fell across her
husband-to-be, and her face lit up. "He redefined my defi-
nition of love, and because of him I'm a more understanding person."

"Good, then give me my sleeping pills!"

Laughing, Sharleen stood and dropped the bottle into
Dionne's outstretched hands.

"Have a good nap."

"I will. See you in an hour." Dionne popped a pill into
her mouth and washed it down with a glass of water. Yawning, she put on her earphones and slipped on her silk sleep
mask. Reclining her seat, she closed her eyes and snuggled in her blanket. As Dionne fell asleep, images of Immanuel filled her mind, and his voice played in her ears
like a love song.

Immanuel was dying to touch Dionne, wanting to reach
out and caress her skin, but he exercised restraint. Dionne
was sleeping peacefully, and he didn't want to disturb her.
Remembering the last time he'd watched her sleep made
his pulse hammer in his ears and an erection rise inside
his boxer briefs. Her perfume was an intoxicating blend
of fruits and flowers, and Immanuel liked the soft, soothing fragrance.

Dionne looked youthful and stylish in her off-the-shoulder blouse, gold accessories and jeans. Her makeup was simple; her hair was in a loose French braid. It had only been two weeks since their breakup, but it felt like months since he'd seen her, and his desire to kiss her was so strong his mouth watered at the sight of her glossy peach lips.

Immanuel tossed aside his business magazine. He wasn't reading it anyway. He'd been watching Dionne for hours, ever since he'd boarded his private plane that morning at ten o'clock, and was so eager to talk to her he couldn't sit still.

Stirring in her seat, she stretched and pulled off her sleep mask. The color drained from her face, and her eyes widened. He sensed her pain, her hurt. Immanuel didn't mean to hurt her, but he had. He wasn't going to lose her. Not today. Not ever. It wasn't too late. He'd fix things. Prove to her that he could be trusted with her heart. She had a beautiful spirit, an energetic, fun-loving personality, and despite the stress of the past few weeks she'd never lost her smile. Loving Dionne was easy, as natural as breathing, and he wanted to be her man.

"Immanuel, what are you doing here?"

"I came to see you. We need to talk."

Dionne glanced around the cabin, then at the side window. "Where is everyone?"

"En route to Venice in Emilio's private plane."

"I thought this *was* his plane."

"No, this is my plane," he said with pride. It was his guilty pleasure, a gift to himself when Mastermind Operations was named business of the year in *Italia Business* magazine. "Once you fell asleep everyone left and boarded Emilio's jet, *Lucca2009*, on runway three."

"You tricked me again! Why?"

"Because I wanted us to be alone."

"There is no us. You ruined *us* when you betrayed me."

His tongue froze inside his mouth. Immanuel didn't know where to start, but he spoke from the heart. Coming clean was therapeutic, the most freeing thing he'd ever done. He told her about his business relationship with Jules, what he'd written in his final report and who was responsible for her attack. Dionne didn't show any emotion when he told her Adeline had hired a man from Detroit to rough her up. "Ask me anything," he implored. "I want to make things right, and I want you to trust me again."

"I appreciate everything you and Malcolm have done for me."

"Adeline won't be bothering you anymore, and if she does she'll be arrested."

"Thank you for telling me the truth, but it doesn't change anything between us," she said, her voice a solemn whisper. "I was married to someone who lied and kept secrets from me for years, and I won't be a fool for love again."

"I was a jerk. Is that what you want to hear?" His palms itched and were damp with sweat. If he could just touch her, kiss her, she'd see what was in his heart and forgive him. He got up, crouched in front of her seat and placed his hands on top of hers. "I was scared of losing you, so I held back. I'm sorry that I hurt you, and I'll never do it again. Going forward, I'll be honest and up-front about everything."

"You should have been honest and up-front from the beginning."

Silence fell across the cabin.

Dionne was staring off into space, acting as if he weren't there, but Immanuel wasn't discouraged. They had plenty of time to work out their problems, and he was confident they'd be a couple again by the time the plane landed in Venice. "Baby, talk to me. What's on your mind?"

"I'm not your baby."

"Yes, you are. You were made for me, and no one else will do." Immanuel studied her, sensing that he was finally making progress, and moved closer to her. "Dionne, I can't live without you. I won't. You're my everything, and I'm nothing without you."

To his relief, her eyes brightened, and a small smile curled her lips.

"No one else compares to you." He took her hands in his and held them to his chest.

"You're a strong, self-made woman who carries herself with poise and grace—"

"That's a lie. I'm not."

Immanuel furrowed his eyebrows. "You're not what? I don't understand."

"I'm not a self-made woman." Hanging her head, she fiddled with the gold ring on her left hand. "I didn't build my business through blood, sweat and tears. My publisher put that in my bio to sell more books, but it isn't true. I used the alimony settlement from my first divorce to buy my office at Peachtree Plaza."

He cupped her chin in his hands, forcing her to meet his gaze. "Why are you ashamed? You've done nothing wrong."

"I feel like a fraud. I'm not a rags-to-riches success story, and I feel guilty for profiting off a lie. "

"You're not, so stop thinking that way. You used your alimony settlement to better yourself and help others, and that's nothing to be ashamed of." He paused. "In my opinion you *are* a self-made woman at the top of her game. And you're hot, too!"

Dionne burst out laughing, and his chest inflated with pride.

"Do you still need a tour guide in Italy?" he asked.

"Yes, Mr. Morretti, as a matter of fact I do. When are you availablc?"

Chuckling, he cupped her cheeks in his hands and showered her lips with kisses. They were sweeter and more addictive than red wine, and he couldn't get enough. "You've made me the happiest man alive!"

Dionne tossed her head back and shrieked with laughter. "You're *so* dramatic!"

"I'm not dramatic. I'm just a man desperately in love."

Surprise splashed across her face.

"How do you say 'I love you' in Somali?"

"Waan ku ieclahav."

"Wow, that's a mouthful," he said good-naturedly. *"Waan ku ieclahav*, Dionne. I love you with all my heart, and I always will, even when I'm old, gray and senile!"

Laughing through her tears, she asked, "How do you say 'I love you' in Italian?"

"Ti amo."

"Ti amo, baby. You're the best thing that's ever happened to me, and all the man I need."

They held each other tight, kissed with an intoxicating blend of tenderness, passion and hunger. Immanuel knew in his heart they'd be together forever. He had everything he'd ever wanted in life—a rewarding career, his family and most important the love of a good woman—and he'd never take his blessings for granted again.

Chapter 21

Palazzo Grassi, the seventeenth-century palace along the Grand Canal in Venice, Italy, was a striking piece of architecture. It was filled with glass chandeliers, contemporary art and paintings, gleaming marble, and wide, Gothic-style windows that offered breathtaking views of the canal. There was something romantic and mysterious about the palace, and the moment she'd entered it she'd fallen under its seductive spell.

Seated inside the ballroom, at the table to the left of the swan ice sculpture, Dionne sipped her red wine. The weekend had been one nonstop party, filled with one surprise after another, and she was having the time of her life with Immanuel and his loud, irreverent family.

Dionne swept her gaze around the room, admiring the striking gold-and-red decor. Soaring floral arrangements were packed with roses and wisteria, and the heady scent inundated the air. Candelabras bathed the room in a soft light, and satin-draped tables were covered with fine china, designer linens and menu cards adorned with Swarovski crystals.

A server in a black couture gown refilled her glass and quickly departed. There was no end to the glamour and grandeur of Sharleen and Emilio's wedding, and as Dionne ate her strawberry soufflé, she reflected on the events of the day. The wedding had been held in the main hall of the palace. The forty-five-minute ceremony was so touching Dionne—and every other female guest—had wept tears of joy. The bride wowed in a tulle mermaid gown with quarter sleeves, and the groom looked dapper in his crisp white tuxedo. Watching the happy couple feeding each other cake at the head table warmed Dionne's heart. Emilio had given Sharleen the wedding of her dreams, and she was thrilled her favorite couple were now husband and wife.

Laughter rang out, and Dionne glanced up from her plate. All across the room, guests decked out in jewels and couture fashion danced, mingled and sipped champagne. Peering around the chocolate fondue tower, she searched the room for Immanuel. Dionne couldn't find him anywhere. Ten minutes earlier, his cousins, Demetri, Nicco and Rafael, had pulled him aside, and she hadn't seen him since. Dionne didn't mind, though. She was having fun visiting with his grandmother, and wondered if all the stories the little old lady had told her about Immanuel's wild teenage years were true.

"Tell us the story again. I just *love* hearing it, especially the part when Immanuel took you in his arms, whisked you away to safety and saved the day…"

Dionne turned to Angela. The TV reporter wasn't the only one with stars in her eyes. Sisters-in-law Jariah and Paris Morretti were sitting on the edge of their seats, too. Since arriving in Venice three days earlier, she'd told the story numerous times, and every time she did Immanuel's grandmother broke down and cried. Being around Gianna made Dionne miss her own grandparents. *Who knows?* she thought, eating the last bite of her dessert. *Maybe Immanuel will come with me to visit them next year.*

Dionne caught herself. She had to introduce Immanuel to her parents before she took him halfway around the world to Somalia. In many ways, he reminded her of her father, and she was confident her two favorite men would hit it off. "I was walking to my car, talking to my cousin on my cell, when I felt someone grab me from behind…"

Eyes wide, her expression filled with terror, Gianna clutched Dionne's hand in a fierce grip.

Dionne finished the story and laughed when the women clapped and cheered.

"Immanuel's such a great guy," Jariah gushed.

"I agree," Dionne said, her heart overcome with love. "Thank God he uncovered the truth, or my ex-sister-in-law would probably still be terrorizing me."

"I think you're great for my grandson, and it's wonderful that you and I are a lot alike."

"We are, Gianna? Really? In what ways?"

"Isn't it obvious?" She winked and fluffed her curls. "We're both smart and sexy!"

Laughing, the women clinked glasses.

Spotting Immanuel at the bar, she put down her fork and dabbed at her lips with her napkin. She wanted to explore the palace, and hoped her handsome boyfriend would take her for a tour of the grounds. Excusing herself from the table, she walked confidently across the room. Dionne felt like a goddess in her beaded floor-length gown and sultry, exotic makeup. Her hair was in a braided bun, adorned with crystals, and Immanuel had been praising her look all night.

"I don't think we've met."

An attractive man with striking eyes and chiseled features appeared at her side. "I'm Dante, the young, wickedly handsome brother of the groom," he said smoothly, his voice carrying the hint of a West Coast accent. "And you are?"

These Morretti men sure have a way with words, she thought, giving him the once-over. *And they're all hot, hot, hot!* She took the hand he offered and smiled when he kissed her on each cheek. "I'm Dionne. It's a pleasure to meet you, Dante."

"A beautiful name for a beautiful woman." Wearing a pensive expression on his face, he stroked his square, chiseled jaw. *"Dante and Dionne* has a nice ring to it, don't you think? We could be the hot new 'it' couple!"

"You're going to have a ring around your *eye* if you don't get away from my girl."

Giggling, Dionne watched as the brothers embraced. All weekend, Immanuel had been introducing her to his relatives, and her head throbbed just thinking about all the people she'd met. Dante was a gregarious, life-of-the-party type, and Dionne liked him immediately.

"Holy crap! *You're* Dionne?"

Taken aback by his reaction, she said, "Yes, I am. Is that a problem?"

"No, it's fine. *You're* fine. In fact, too beautiful for him." Dante gave Immanuel a shot in the ribs with his elbow. "You know she's way out of your league, right?"

"Hater!" Immanuel winked at Dionne, then offered his arm. "May I have this dance?"

Nodding, she clasped his forearm and followed him to the dance floor. It was crowded with hundreds of guests, but they found a spot and wrapped their arms around each other. The song playing was in Italian. Dionne didn't know what it was about, but she loved the way it made her feel. Excited, aroused, in the mood for passionate, sensuous lovemaking.

"I'm going to ravish you from head to toe when we get back to my hotel suite."

Dionne fluttered her eyelashes and wore an innocent smile. "Why wait?"

"You're such a naughty girl," he said with a grin. "Whatever shall I do with you?"

"I'm sure you'll think of something. You always do."

"What's next?"

Glancing at the head table, Dionne remembered the conversation she'd had with Sharleen earlier in the powder room, and said, "The garter toss, the bouquet toss and…"

"No, not tonight. What's next for us?"

"Isn't this conversation a little premature? We've only been dating a few weeks."

"No, not to me. I'm turning forty in June, and all I want for my birthday is you," Immanuel said. "How does a summer wedding in Venice sound?"

Dionne took a moment to sort her thoughts and consider her words. They were having a great time together, and she didn't want to do anything to hurt his feelings, but they were moving too fast. "I've had two failed marriages, and if I get married again I want it to be forever."

"Not *if* you get married again, *when*." His gaze met hers, held her in its strong, seductive grip. "You know what they say. Third time's the charm."

"I have a history of plunging headfirst into relationships, and I think that's why I've never had success with the opposite sex. This time around, I want to take things slow."

"How slow are we talking? As my grandmother so kindly pointed out this morning at breakfast, I'm not getting any younger," he joked, stroking her shoulders. "If I proposed to you on Valentine's Day, what would you say?"

"That's less than two months away."

"You didn't answer the question."

Dionne was conflicted, unsure of what to say, and struggled to put her feelings into words. "Baby, I love you, but I'm scared of being a three-time loser in the game of love. What if we get married and things don't work out? What if we fall out of love, and—"

"That's impossible. We're destined to be together, and I'll never, *ever* leave you."

"I want us to date for a year before we get engaged."

"A year? That's a long time."

Dionne laughed and shook her head at him. "Paris told me Morretti men waste no time putting a ring on it, and she was right!"

They laughed together, then shared a soft, sweet kiss on the lips.

"I'm glad you turned down that TV deal," he confessed, openly sharing his feelings. "Now I don't have to compete with celebrities for your time."

Dionne nodded her head in understanding. Yesterday, while reclining by the hotel pool, the TV producer had called and offered her a job on his reality show, and she'd surprised herself and Immanuel by turning him down. Dionne wanted to grow her business, but she didn't want to work twelve-hour days or travel four days a week; she wanted to spend her free time with Immanuel and no one else. "To be honest, it was an easy decision to make."

"If you want to take things slow, then that's what we'll do." Immanuel held her close to his chest. "Baby, you're my everything, and I'll do anything to make you happy."

Love shone in his eyes, warmed his face with happiness. Peace filled her, silencing her fears and doubts. Dionne knew then, as Immanuel kissed her, she'd finally found her soul mate, a strong, sensitive hero who'd love and protect her until the end of time.

* * * * *

REQUEST YOUR FREE BOOKS!

2 FREE NOVELS
PLUS 2 FREE GIFTS!

KIMANI™
ROMANCE

Love's ultimate destination!

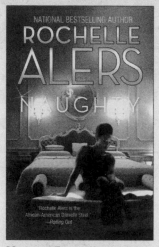